L967u

The Un-Dudding of Roger Judd

ALSO BY HARRIETT LUGER

Chasing Trouble
The Elephant Tree
Lauren

The Un-Dudding of Roger Judd

BY HARRIETT LUGER

The Viking Press, New York

First Edition
Copyright © 1983 by Harriett Mandelay Luger
All rights reserved
First published in 1983 by The Viking Press
40 West 23rd Street, New York, New York 10010
Published simultaneously in Canada by Penguin Books Canada Limited
Printed in U.S.A.
1 2 3 4 5 87 86 85 84 83

Library of Congress Cataloging in Publication Data
Luger, Harriett Mandelay.   The un-dudding of Roger Judd.
Summary: Sixteen-year-old Californian Roger, unhappy with himself
and his life since his father's remarriage, goes to visit his mother, a
recovered alcoholic, in New York City, where he has a revelation that
changes his life.
[1. Remarriage—Fiction. 2. Family problems—Fiction] I. Title.
PZ7.L97814Un 1983 [Fic] 82–50362 ISBN 0–670–73886–7

*To Isaac and David Luger
and Rachel Slayback*

The Un-Dudding of Roger Judd

Saturday, February 3

I am one helluva guy.

Me, Roger Richard Judd. The guy who lives at 2001 Ernest Avenue, Del Amo, California, 90803.

Faced off two—not one, but *two*—big ugly slobs with .22s. No backup. Not even my dog Pippa. And that girl was no help. Got me into the mess, then jumped behind me when they aimed at us.

And who ran away? Not Roger Judd—but the slobs with the .22s!

Just one helluva guy! Me, Roger Judd the Dud, Mr. Nobody of Central High!

I sure wish I had someone to tell. I wish I could tell Dad, but he and Lou were already in the car backing out when I got home. She rolled down the window, told me that my dinner was in the fridge, and he gave me a wave, and off they went. If I can catch him without Vanessa or Lou hanging all over him tomorrow, I'll tell him. I can't wait to inform him that his son is one helluva hero. It will be news to him.

So this is what happened. It plays better every time I roll it. I get a charge out of reliving every single minute.

I was taking Pippa to the field. I forgot her leash, and she made me chase her for half a block before I could get my hand through her collar. The coyote in her gives her character and slanted eyes and a pretty face, but you can't tame her. So I had to crouch lopsided all the way to the field to hang on to her so she wouldn't kill herself in traffic chasing a cat.

She is a hunter, and she'd die under the wheels of a car rather than let her prey get away.

We got to the field—a mile of space and weeds and rabbits and gophers and mice surrounded by Southern California traffic. Shallow groves of eucalyptus trees along Maple and Crenshaw, the short sides. Scattered oil pumps inside chain-link squares, connected by dirt roads. Telephone poles. A railway spur along the north side, way up by the edge, but the trains don't come often enough to worry about. This is Pippa's territory. This is where she comes alive.

She streaked off down the road that parallels Sepulveda, with me following in my usual mood, head down, hands in pockets. I was wondering about Everett Simms, who O.D.'d on Valium and booze last weekend, and the word around school is that it was no accident. He was in some of my classes. A Junior like me. Quiet guy in no trouble anyone knew about. Everyone was surprised. Maybe he didn't know how to be happy. Or maybe he figured life is just not worth the trouble. Maybe he looked around and decided it's healthier to be dead. I mean, nukes all over the place waiting for the button, carcinogens floating around so you can't breathe or take a drink of water and be sure you aren't killing yourself. I mean, living is dangerous to your health, man.

I looked up and saw Pippa playing with a low-slung white dog and some kid in a red jacket up ahead of me. Then I forgot about them when I noticed a big red-tailed hawk sitting on a telephone pole cross-arm, focusing its gaze on me like a laser beam. I beamed back a message of peace and goodwill so I could get close enough to see its mean curved beak and hawk eye. But as usual, when I was about fifty, sixty feet away, it flew off the pole and into the air. I tipped my head back and watched the strong wings—I bet they were four feet across, with feathers like fingers at the ends—climb the air. The stubby red tail, spread like a fan, caught the sun as the hawk scudded with the wind, tacked against it, went into a quick, steep climb, then into a perfect roll, turning completely over, then floated down to the top of another pole toward the middle of the field.

I start walking again. The red-jacketed figure is running toward me. It has bouncing breasts, so I know it's a girl. The dogs circle and jump at her. She is clutching her head with both hands, squeaking in distress. I think to myself, Crap, what now?

"They're shooting at the hawk!" she squeaks, pointing to a tall shrub rising above the weeds. I see two heads almost hidden in the foliage, and two gun barrels aimed at the telephone pole. They are too far away for a good shot. I am not worried about the hawk, and no way do I intend to get involved. But Pippa has spotted them and takes off, bounding toward them through the weeds like a deer. She is an imbecile. Real cautious when we put out her food, circling her dish, creeping up on it as if she expected it to bite—but she considers any stranger her good buddy. The short-legged dog follows, rocking through and around the plants, because he can't go over them the way she can.

So these two big hulking goons about my age come out of the tree. Each has a .22, which he swings at Pippa, but she thinks they're playing and dances on her hind legs. She jumps up on the bigger one, who almost catches her on the side of the head with his rifle stock. The hawk flies away. I whistle.

I yell. That stupid dog has gone stone-deaf, but the guys hear me. They give me that blank macho look that says mess with us at your own risk, buddy.

I hear this strange, hoarse, off-key voice coming from me: "The oil company guys'll radio for the cops if they see your guns."

"What for? What're we doing?" the tall one asks.

"Shooting red-tails," the girl squeaks. She has followed me. I sense right away that she is scared and that she is the kind that never knows when to keep her mouth shut. I move away from her to make it clear she's not my girl friend, that I don't even know her.

"Anyway, it's gone," I croak but nobody hears. The guys are ogling the girl, their eyes horny.

"So what's wrong with shooting red-tails?" the shorter one asks. Shorter, ha-ha. They are both Rams linesman material. And I'm good chess material. Five six, one hundred and twenty-three pounds.

"Why do you have to shoot at it? What's it ever done to you?" the girl asks in a shaky squeak.

"What's it ever done to me?" The tall one grins at his buddy. "It's what hawks do to bunnies." He leers at the girl. "Don't you like bunnies?"

"Him and me are bunny lovers. Him and me belong to the Bunny Lovers of America," the short one says, and they crack up. A tear rolls down the girl's cheek, and her fists are clenched, but she keeps looking at the guys.

Desperately I clear my throat and croak again, "Anyway, it's not here any more. It's gone."

At that moment Pippa sashays up to the big guy, giving

him all kinds of love messages. "What kind of mutt is he?" the guy asks. I tell him part coyote, part husky. "Coyote." He smirks at his partner. "Another bunny killer." He raises his rifle to his shoulder and sights at her point-blank as she flirts and prances. The girl screams and grabs her head.

I yell, "Cut it out!" and push the gun barrel aside.

"Take your hands off my gun," the big guy tells me.

"Then don't point it at my dog." The croak splits to high C on "dog."

"Nobody touches my gun!"

We lock eyeballs. They stand shoulder to shoulder, looking down at me. I take in the ugly faces, the thick necks, massive shoulders—and the rifles. The closest street is half a mile away. The whole entire field is empty except for us. The situation is pitiful.

"Looking for trouble?" the short one asks.

"Wanna get wasted?" the big one says, giving me the cold fish eye.

"Try it." The voice peeps like a piccolo.

They aim their guns at us. The girl screams and scoots behind me, and there I am rooted to the ground, a stationary target, big as life.

That was the longest second in my life. No lie! The weeds stand stock-still. Not one bird utters a peep. The dogs sit, interested, Pippa looking as if she's trying to decide whether to go with those gorillas or stick with me. Their eyes shift to something behind me, and the short one says, "Crap! Here comes an oil truck," and they run away through the weeds where the truck can't follow, but when it passes without changing speed on its way to the drilling tower near Crenshaw, they turn around and flip us off, then disappear into the railroad cut.

My legs feel like rubber. I want to sit down and hang my head between my knees, but that dumb, stupid, squeaky female is looking at me, squeaking again.

"They could have killed us! They pointed their guns right at us!"

"Yes, and the damn hawk flew away while you were flapping your gums! Didn't you see it fly away? Didn't you hear me say that it flew away? You almost got me shot, you and your big mouth!"

Actually, it was Pippa who got me into this mess, but I did not appreciate the girl's jumping behind me. Why should I get shot instead of her? I turn on my heel and leave without calling Pippa. As far as I'm concerned Pippa can go with those gorillas or she can get herself smeared all over Sepulveda Boulevard for all I care. I know if she comes near me, I'll kick her.

For once she follows without being called. So does the other dog and the girl, as if they were all imprinted on me. The girl is almost crying.

"I'm sorry. I didn't mean to get you in trouble—I didn't mean to jump behind you. I was so scared—when they aimed at me I thought they were going to kill me!"

"But it was O.K. for them to kill me!" I yell.

She was really crying now. "I didn't mean to—but when he pointed that gun, my legs jumped—I had nothing to do with it. Honest, I didn't mean to—I was just scared, and you were so great. Two of them—great big slobs!"

That's when it hit me.

Roger Judd the Dud stood up to not one but two genuine slob gorillas—with .22s! "Try it," I told them. I actually said that, and *they* split and nothing happened to me! How about that! Forget that I couldn't control my voice and that I was shaking like a belly dancer and that the oil truck bailed me out. I stood up to those slobs and looked them in the eye and told them off! Even when I was on the receiving end of a gun barrel, I was on my feet, looking them in the eye. Maybe I ought to rethink this Dud garbage.

Only I wish I could have told Dad.

No way am I going to put this in that rinky-dink journal we have to keep for English (which is why I have this notebook in the first place), so that Old Lady Baker can comb through it for spelling errors and dangling participles. She'd probably come up with something like, "This journal is supposed to be factual, not fictional." So I'll just write something like, "I took my dog for a walk and we saw a hawk"—something like that.

There is no connection between one day and the next. There never is. Good days, bad days, no matter what you do or don't do. Yesterday was like finding a twenty-dollar bill. I wasn't looking for it, didn't work for it—it just happened. But a twenty-dollar bill doesn't make you rich.

So on the way home from the field I stopped at Clark's Drugs and bought another $8\frac{1}{2} \times 11$ spiral binder that I'm going to use for the school journal. In this one I'm going to write what happens to me for the next month, maybe two months. Lay it on the line in black-and-white. Everything— good, bad, whatever. Then I'm going to take a good, hard look at my life and see if I can make any sense out of it. When I look ahead at all the time I have to fill with my screwups and failures before I get to be an old man, on top of watching the planet go to hell and people killing each other, I wonder if I shouldn't get out while I'm still ahead.

Only it's so damn final. No round trip. Strictly no refund, no return, baby.

But if I do kill myself—which I'm not 110 percent sold on doing—I want my parents to know why and who to blame. I will leave this journal to them. It will give them a thing or two to think about. My mom in New York will take it hard, and she has this drinking problem, so for her sake I guess I shouldn't. My father's blood pressure would shoot up fifty points, but he'll be better off in the long run. If I stick around, I'll probably give him a heart attack.

So what happened to cut the big hero down to size?

This morning I was standing by the sink eating breakfast. I started to tell Dad about the two goons, but he was talking at the same time. Wanted me to help him in the garage, and why didn't I sit down and eat like a normal person, and he was out the back door before I could get a word in edgewise. I figured I'd catch him in the garage.

Then Vanessa came over to the sink, crowding me. She's been doing that lately, brushing, pushing against me. She said, "Move, I need a drink." She filled a glass from the faucet and swallowed with loud, slow swallows, watching me without blinking. I stared back. We always have this contest to see whose eyeballs dry up first. Still without a blink, she said, "Have you ever kissed a girl, Roger?"

She knows how many girls I know, let alone kiss. But I kept my eyes on hers, even though I felt myself get red. Kind of giggling, she slowly leaned across me, put the glass on the drainboard, crowding me, breathing on my neck, pressing her breast against my bare arm. The big hero went into shock. He dropped his glass into the sink. It shattered into a hundred pieces.

That slime Vanessa. I hate her guts. She giggled, "God, you're clumsy. How come you're so clumsy?" Then she bounced out of the kitchen, leaving me hating myself for not grabbing her and kissing her or belting her or both.

I went out to the garage, sucking my finger, which I had cut digging glass out of the garbage disposal. I started shifting stuff with one hand. We're getting ready to move in the summer. We've been here a year and a half, Dad and I. This place belongs to Lou, the woman he married. Dental hygienist. It comes from her first marriage, like her slimy sixteen-year-old daughter, Vanessa. The place on the hill is bigger, has a pool and hot tub. Good investment. Big deal. Just another move as far as I'm concerned.

I was fuming, confused that something as fantastic as a breast should belong to that slime Vanessa, so I guess I wasn't working very fast. Dad barked at me to get a Band-Aid so he could have the benefit of both my hands. My finger had stopped bleeding, so I stopped sucking and used both hands to jockey cartons and trunks, waiting to calm down before telling him about yesterday. Before I had a chance, he asked if I was doing better in chemistry. I grunted and shrugged. Actually, I don't know how I'm doing in chemistry. I haven't been there all week. I'm also slowly sinking in English—something he doesn't know yet. This is the worst I've ever done in school. He thought my shrug and grunt meant that everything was under control.

He said, "That's more like it. If Vanessa can do it, you can do it. You're as sharp as she is."

That set me off. "Can't you see what a phony she is?"

"If being a phony means being alive and getting good grades and keeping yourself sharp and having friends, I want you to be that kind of phony. Vanessa tells me you don't have one friend at school. She never sees you hanging around with anyone—"

"Now she's spying on me!" I yelled. "What else did she tell you about me?" I was frantic that he would find out how many classes I've cut.

"Nobody's spying on you! She merely said you're a loner, you don't have any friends—damn it, I worry about you!"

Then he goes into his old routine. When he was sixteen, he had a crowd of kids he ran around with, he had a girl friend, he was pumping gas and paying his father for his first jalopy. "Lots of kids work. I have one working for me right now at VID."

"Why doesn't *she* have to get a job?" I ask.

"As a matter of fact, she's got a job lined up at Tinker's Tacos. She's going to start as soon as they reorganize. But forget about her. We're talking about you."

It's hopeless. I'll give anyone twenty-to-one odds she never gets that job. She won't even try hard for it. She's a con artist, and it kills me that he can't see it.

Now I didn't even want to tell him about those gorillas. I began to wonder if it was such a big deal, anyway. I didn't fight them or anything. I just wanted to get as far away as possible from this house and him and Vanessa. So I let him rave for a while, then asked if I could have the van this afternoon. But Vanessa had it reserved.

"She always has it or she has it reserved," I yelled. "Why can't she use Lou's car?"

Well, Lou had to grocery shop, and why did I always wait till the last minute and then get my nose out of joint? Or better yet, if I got a job so I could pay for my gas, he'd buy me a car. Totally unrealistic but unanswerable. If I had asked him who's going to hire a wimp, a geek, a dud, he would have told me to stop feeling sorry for myself. He doesn't understand. And sometimes I wonder if he cares.

I yanked a decrepit little old carton that came with us from our real home with Mom and Dad to all the apartment garages to here. It stuck, and I yanked again and tore a big piece out of one of the sides, and a lot of small junk spilled all over the floor. Dad jerked around, startled, and knocked a bottle of battery water off the bench. All the little screws and washers and nails and drill bits were swimming. He got heart-attack red and blew up.

"Can't you do anything right? You're no help! You just make more work! Get out of here and leave me alone. Take a hike! Beat it!"

I cleared out. I got Pippa's leash and went to the field. I had no place else. I never did get a chance to tell Dad about me and those guys. I can't believe him. After six years of just him and me since Mom left. O.K., I'm not much, but I never gave him any trouble, and he wasn't all that great to live with—grouchy as hell, short fuse—but I understood him. I tried not to make his blood pressure go up. And we had ball games and shows and camping and the trip down the Colorado. And Pippa since four years ago.

Then, zap, everything changed. If yesterday was like finding a twenty-dollar bill, October thirteenth a year before last was like being wiped out of every cent. No warning. I'll never forget the day, the minute, the second. We were on that hillside in Palos Verdes, one of those they're now leveling and turning into condominiums. Pippa was off chasing skunks or rattlesnakes or something, and Dad and I were walking along a path through dry, yellow weeds, and he said to me, "Roger, Lou and I are getting married."

"Why?" I asked, stopping dead in my tracks. "What do you want to go and do that for?"

"I like her. She likes me. We want to be together."

"What about me?"

"I've thought about you, Roger. I've thought a lot about you. You need a home—all those years of baby sitters or coming home to an empty apartment and watching TV—it'll be good for you to have a real home and someone your own age to be around. You've been alone too much—" He stammered all the way through. The first time I've ever heard my father stammer. He wasn't sure I was going to like this marriage, but he was going through with it, anyway.

"But we're doing fine, man," I said desperately.

"She's a good person, Roger," he said, kind of pleading. "Once you get to know her, you'll like her a lot. And Vanessa's fun—" Fun like cancer. Already then I had that feeling about her.

I tried to reason with him. "But we don't *need* them. Why can't you see Lou the way you see your other girl friends? Why do you have to marry her?"

He blew up. "Because I want to, damn it! Don't you think six long years is enough for a guy to carry the whole load himself? Six long, tough years?"

I'd had no idea that the years were *that* long or *that* tough for him. Maybe if I had been more of a winner, sharper, better at sports, wheeler-dealer—something—but he was a rotten traitor. Selling me out for a stinking cuddle bunny. More like a cuddle cow. I'll never forgive him.

Who should I run into today as I was leaving English but that girl. Turned out she was waiting for Carmel Bierre. The minute I saw them together, I knew they were sisters. Both small, dark-haired, dark-eyed. Only Carmel is a real beauty.

The girl started squeaking at me about how she's checked out every oversize nerd at Central High, and those slobs with the rifles don't go here. She asked me my name, and I told her, trying to edge away, but she followed, squeaking non-stop. Man, is she a talker. Her name is Julie Bierre, and Carmel is her twin, and she is totally sick with shame for using me as a shield.

"Honest to God, Roger, I didn't mean to. It was my central nervous system or my endocrine system or something. Just took over—"

I kept saying, "That's O.K.," trying to shake her, but she stuck like glue. I had to lead her to a Boy's and duck in to get rid of her. She was still talking.

What a pest. Funny, it never occurred to me that I would ever see the goons again. Then what kind of hero would I have been? A plastered hero—plastered all over the landscape.

Why couldn't it have been Carmel in the field Saturday? With her in Julie's place and me cool and tight, and we start going together and find out we're made for each other. She'd never go for a creep like me—but what if she *had* been there Saturday instead of squeaky? How can she go for a total zero like Gene Merriam? Come to think of it, where is Gene Merriam? Haven't seen him around for a couple of weeks now.

Tuesday, February 6

No matter what Dad and Vanessa and Lou think about me, Saturday afternoon actually did happen. They don't know me. I used to think Dad did, but I guess he was having too tough a time to think about me. Now he's too busy playing with Lou and Vanessa. None of them see me as I really am. A first-class 24-carat hero. So for the past two days I have been going to all my classes looking everyone in the eye. The impact is less than zero, but what the hell.

I got the brilliant idea of using one Disaster Data item every day for my school journal. Yesterday I wrote about "Nuclear Radiation: A Deadly Fact of Life" and today about "Buildup of Carbon Dioxide in the Atmosphere May Change World's Climate." That ought to go over big with Old Lady Baker. Roger Judd, Concerned Environmentalist. Which is not entirely fake. I am concerned. I can hardly stand to watch what's happening to the planet.

Wednesday, February 14

Happy Valentine's Day. Vanessa gave Dad a little heart-shaped box with about six chocolates in it, and he fell apart thanking her. Practically fell down on the floor and kissed her big fat feet. Then she asked him for the van to go to Jennifer's. She had it yesterday, too. Lou had to go to a meeting. Last night it was shopping. I told him I had to go to the library, I have a report due. He asked when, and like a fool I told him the truth—a week from next Monday. He said I can have it tomorrow night or else walk to the library. So I asked why couldn't she walk to Jennifer's. Because they don't want her walking alone at night. But it's all right for me to walk alone at night. I'm no bigger than she is. What about my equal rights?

And she was standing behind his chair pointing those things at me and giving me the stare while he went into his spiel. When he was my age he was paying for his own jalopy, etc. etc. She got impatient and mouthed, "Who cares?", then she kissed the top of his head, and he handed over the keys, and she said, "Thank you, Jack," and went out, bouncing all over, and I almost threw up. She calls him Jack instead of Sterling, which is his name. It's a big joke between them.

After she left, he said, "It would have been nice if you had bought a little something for Lou." I told him I can't be a phony like Vanessa. He got heart-attack red and started yelling that he's tired of this phony crap. Here's a nice, friendly, attractive girl I should be friends with instead of hostile to—blah, blah.

I walked out on him and came up to my room. If I had wheels I could get away from all this. I would roll along on the 405 past Long Beach doing eighty-five, ninety, roll along on my big tires, smooth, man, weaving in and out, passing everybody, in control, nobody hassling me. If it was too hot, turn on the air conditioning. If it was too cold, turn on the heater. Just steer and listen to my tapes. Peace, man, peace.

Wouldn't you know that something that great is garbaging up the atmosphere with hydrocarbons.

My father just left my room. Came up to see me. Stood at the foot of my bed, looking at me, looking at my room, looking at his hands. We just can't talk any more. Finally he said he wished I wouldn't be so hostile to Lou and Vanessa. Can't we discuss it? I asked what there was to discuss.

"Why don't you give them a chance?" he blurted out, getting red, trying to keep his temper. I shrugged. More silence. Then he said he knew I was having a hard time adjusting to his marriage, but it's been a year and a half now, and I'm sixteen years old, and it's time for me to do something for myself instead of mope and sulk. Make friends, get a job, he doesn't care what kind. He doesn't care if I finish up this year with only a C average. (He should only know.) He'll meet me halfway and get me a car of my own if I just get off my duff and show some initiative. And a job would help him—if I paid some of my own expenses—because money is getting tight. I promise to try.

What difference does it make, anyway? We'll all be nuked one of these days before we can die of starvation or cancer. All of us—the jocks, the brains, the movers and shakers, and the duds like me.

Thursday, February 22

Rain all week. Still coming down. On TV I have been watching California melting away. Hills sagging, houses sliding into canyons. The field is one soggy mess. Everything drips.

I got a 53 on a chem quiz today, and Fretter had a serious talk with me. Said I need a tutor, to speak to my father about it, and if he agrees, Fretter will recommend one. But I'm going to hit the books double hard from now on to see if I can't pull myself up. I just can't face telling Dad. I have a book report due Monday and haven't even read the damn book. Also I'm about a week behind on my journal. I have the Disaster Data items cut out, but I don't just copy them into the journal, I kinda write them up in my own scintillating style.

This afternoon between rains I figured I ought to take Pippa for a quick run. She hasn't been out of the yard for a week. As soon as we got to the field she streaked away, and I knew I wouldn't see her again till she was good and ready. The road that parallels Sepulveda is damp but drained, up to that pond that is nothing but a big pothole till it rains. I was picking my way in the muck around it, concentrating on not falling on my ass and noticing how six inches of water in a pothole traps all of eternity—you know, the reflection of the sky—so I did not see Julie until it was too late. She was planted right in my way, blushing, not looking at me, but not moving.

"Listen"—her voice wobbled—"this is the last time I'm going to bug you, but I've got to say it. My self-respect is down to here." She bent down, holding her hand near the ground. "I'm having a hard time living with myself."

"That's O.K.," I mumbled, wishing she'd disappear, vanish, go away.

"I'm so ashamed of myself—" She couldn't go on for snuffling, and I thought to myself, Oh, crap, she's going to cry.

"Forget it. I was scared blind myself," I told her.

"But you didn't duck behind me."

"You were too fast. Greased lightning." She laughed a weepy, snuffly laugh. To change the subject, I said, "I didn't know you were Carmel Bierre's sister." She told me Carmel was born half an hour sooner, weighed half a pound more, got all the goodies, and she, Julie, got the leftovers. I didn't know what to answer, because it's true.

For a while we watched the dogs, who were having hysterics at meeting each other again. Suddenly Pippa checked herself in mid-leap and began sniffing a tuft of weed. Julie's dog, whose name is Butchie and who looks like a fat white sausage on legs, right away got serious, too, and they gave that weed one hell of a smelling. Then they both lifted their legs. Pippa marks that way sometimes; sometimes she squats like a girl. I have always figured she was confused because she had been spayed before she knew who she really was.

"It pees like a female coyote. Is it a girl?" Julie said.

That was the last thing I expected her to say. I asked how a female coyote pees. "Lifts her leg with the foot pointed forward like your dog does instead of back like male dogs and male coyotes."

It turned out she read this book about coyotes. I told her our vet says Pippa is cocker spaniel and collie, but I don't believe it. The guy we got her from said she was coyote and husky, and she just doesn't behave like any ordinary dog. Julie said this woman who wrote the book practically lived with coyotes. She ought to know. We watched Pippa skimming down the road, followed by Butchie, who moved like a rocking horse. "She runs like a coyote," Julie said.

Pippa wheeled around and came charging back, swerving around us right smack into the puddle, making a big splashing, barking, biting at the water, causing toads to jump out in all directions. A lot of them were piggyback, hugging each other, one on top of the other, as if they were glued together. I made a grab for a pair in the muck at the edge of the water, but, without separating, they plopped into the pond. Julie cornered a pair against a clump of wet weeds. As she slowly reached for them, they went straight up in the air, still stuck together. She finally trapped them against a rock, puffed up and glaring. She picked them up, but when they began to pee, she handed them to me.

"Here. Have a couple of horny toads."

That cracked me up. You know—toads that are horny, not horny toad lizards—we laughed like crazy. I turned them upside down. The male was hanging on to the female with three perfect little fingers pressed on her chest where her breasts would be if she were a woman. Only, I didn't see how he could do anything because his folded legs rested on her back, and I couldn't find his penis. "I wonder how he gets the job done," I said.

"She lays the eggs in a string of jelly in the water, and that's when he does his thing, on the jelly," Julie said. I remembered something called external fertilization from biology.

"Poor guy, what does he get out of it?" I said, looking at the puffed-up toads. They glared back at me. I tried to pry them apart.

"Leave them alone. They're crazy about each other. They're madly, passionately in love. Stop bugging them," Julie said. So I squatted by the pond and dropped them into the water. "Good-bye and good luck," I said.

We turned back to Maple, milking that gag about the horny toads, which I still think is pretty funny. All of a sudden we heard this ungodly screaming. "Butchie! Where are you?" Julie yelled, plunging into the wet weeds, with me following.

Butchie sounded as if he were losing a leg an inch at a time. Pippa was yapping in falsetto, which meant she had cornered something. In the weeds toward the middle of the field we caught a glimpse of her waving tail and an occasional low-slung flash of white.

The dogs had this gopher between them, and Pippa, still yapping, was feinting and darting at it, gradually closing in. Butchie, baying in high soprano, kept his distance, but he cut off the gopher's escape in that direction. Both dogs wagged their tails as if it were all in fun, but the gopher knew better. It faced first one, then the other, chattering, squealing, cussing. I was afraid it would grab Pippa by the nose with those long, ugly teeth and hang on. Gophers do that.

Of course those mutts paid no attention to us. I kicked at Pippa. She dodged. Then, faster than I could see, she sprang and seized the gopher by the neck, shaking it the way she shakes sticks, playfully arching her neck, prancing, always shaking. She dropped the gopher, nuzzled it, licked it all over gently, as if she were kissing it. I hoped it wasn't dead, after all, but she bit off its head and ate it. Then she lipped the rest of the carcass sort of carelessly, turned tail, and disappeared into the weeds. Just like that.

Meanwhile, Butchie crept to neck-stretching distance of what was left, sniffing cautiously, ready to split at any time.

"He's afraid of it," Julie said. "He's a coward like me. He's even afraid of mice." She squatted by the scrap of fur, shooing Butchie away. "Poor little thing," she murmured.

It started to drizzle. I found a flat rock with an edge to it and started digging a hole. Julie crooned, "Look at how it's made, so small, so perfect." She inspected the claws. "Look at how the fur collects raindrops like diamonds." She stroked the pelt. "Feel how soft, Roger."

I squatted next to her, taking from her the limp scrap of fur with the raw, red stump where the head should have been. I inspected a claw, large in proportion to the rest of the corpse, but lying over my finger, it was small, the tough digging nails almost delicate. It had lost its purpose. Useless. For some weird reason I flashed on my own hands, pale, limp, without purpose, folded on my chest.

"Man, this thing is really dead," I said.

"I hope it was old. I hope it wasn't on the verge of its first loving, or a mother with children waiting for it. I hope it was old and tired." Julie stroked the pelt for a second, then continued. "I think the saddest thing that can happen is to die young. I guess that's why I jumped behind you." Then she caught herself and got all flustered. "Which was a lousy, selfish thing to do, because your life is worth as much to you—"

I went back to digging the grave without answering, not sure my life is worth as much to me as hers is to her. I was churning with bitterness and loneliness. She thought I was sore at her. "Me and my big, dumb mouth," she said. I dug furiously for a few minutes, then tossed away the flat rock.

"This is deep enough. Actually I don't know why we're bothering. Some dog or cat is going to dig it up," I said, laying the gopher in the hole.

Julie said, "It shows respect." We both plopped scoops of mud into the hole.

"A fat lot of good respect is going to do it. It's dead," I said.

She said earnestly, "Oh, the respect is for us, because we know that he was a perfect, beautiful little gopher with guts. He stood up to the dogs the way you stood up to those slobs with guns. Only, he didn't even know he was brave . . . he didn't know anything except how to be a gopher."

She's weird.

By the time I got the gopher buried, the rain was coming down hard, and we ran to Maple. She went north on Maple, and of course I went south.

But it's true. The gopher and I didn't go roaring around looking for trouble, but once we found it—or it found us— we stood on our feet and spit in its eye. No matter what Vanessa thinks or Dad or what a nobody I am at school—I didn't knuckle under to those muscleheads.

Thursday, March 1

Mind blower. Carmel is pregnant.

Of course it has to be Merriam, and he's really gone. Vanished. She has been looking crummy lately, only it didn't register on me till today.

I was walking along the road in the field, deep in my misery as usual. I would have seen them before I heard them, but I had my head down, stewing about last night—110 percent injustice. Had my time chart of English dramatists from Marlowe through Shaw that I should have turned in Monday spread out on the dinette table, working on it. Lou was getting dinner ready, and Dad was in the kitchen, too. They must have been messing around because Vanessa swept in, saying this was no time to be sexy, wasn't dinner ready?, she was starved. Then she bounced over and started taking my stuff off the table. I told her to keep her hands off, and we had a fight, and Dad tried to make me apologize, but I locked myself in my room without dinner and starved till they all went to bed.

So today I was walking along the road that skirts the Maple Street eucalyptus grove, seething, hating the whole world, mostly hating myself for being a creep, because if I weren't a creep, they wouldn't treat me like a creep. I heard this high-pitched voice that I recognized immediately.

"Oh, Carmel, what are you going to do?"

I looked up and saw them leaning against one of the trees, pulling at the bark. Carmel was crying. She said, "Have an abortion, if I don't kill myself first!"

At that second they became aware of me. Big shock all around. I looked at my feet.

Julie said unenthusiastically, "Hi, Roger." I didn't answer.

I glanced at Carmel, who had her back to me. I began to walk away, then I turned and said, "I won't talk."

Julie smiled, and it was like a thousand-watt lamp turned on. She said, "I know," and then the light went out, and she looked again as if she were about to cry. The one I really feel sorry for is Carmel. How could she go for Merriam, who is not only a jerk, but a rat, also?

Wednesday, March 7

I stared at the back of Carmel's head all through English today. I wonder when she's going to have the abortion. She sure is no beauty any more. Kind of sallow, and her eyes are dull with dark half-moons under them. Only her nose is still perfect. Julie's tends to spread. Carmel is in my territory now—Miseryland. How about that as a basis for a relationship?

> Welcome to Miseryland, my love.
> May I adore your nose, your nose, your
> beautiful nose?
> Package deal, baby. All or nothing.
> Where the nose goes, so go the ears,
> the butt, and the toes.
> No problem, my love, my dove. I
> can accommodate your ears and your
> toes,
> Your butt and your nose and everything
> in between.

But she doesn't need me. She and Julie are always with a bunch of kids. Not the Big Time Operators like Vanessa and Darrell and that crowd, but a group that hangs out together and laughs a lot. Only lately she and Julie and one other girl have been eating by themselves. I wonder when she's scheduled to have it done. When the abortion is over, that's the end of her problem. Mine has no beginning, no end, because I *am* the problem.

The journals were due today. I had no entries since 2/15, but I turned it in anyway. Maybe Baker'll give me half credit.

Baker had a talk with me today. Asked me why I didn't turn in a complete journal. Told me I'm on thin ice. I'm supposed to keep a journal for another month. More DD. Today I read that a bunch of shrinks are having a conference in Beverly Hills on teenage suicide. They say it's epidemic. Then on the next page I read about this kid who killed his best friend and himself. The friend had made out a will and held a Bible in his hand. Of course I didn't use that. It isn't environmental or political. Will use "U.S. May Place Chemical Warheads in Europe."

Thursday, March 15

Ate lunch with Julie today. I was in the food line, and this ridiculous voice chirped, "Hi, Roger," right behind me, and there she was at my elbow, blushing and radiating at me. I wish she would go radiate somewhere else. She makes me nervous. Then she screeched across half a dozen people to tell the girl she and Carmel usually eat with that she was going to eat with me today. Everybody in her crowd was looking at me, probably wondering who is that nerd? Most of them are in my classes, but probably this is the first time they've ever noticed me. There was no way I could escape this time, and besides, I was curious about Carmel. She was absent from English three times this week, including today.

I followed Julie to an empty table. "Where's Carmel?" I asked when we got settled.

"Home."

"Did she, has she—" I mumbled.

Julie shook her head.

"When is she going to get it done?" I asked.

"A week from tomorrow." Julie chewed on her hamburger, with a long face. "She didn't get up at all today. My mom thinks she has a virus. She should only know. Carmel throws up every morning and misses most of her classes because she's crying in the rest room. Says she's going to kill herself. Marcy—that's her friend, the one we eat with—Marcy and I are afraid to leave her alone."

"It was Gene Merriam, wasn't it?"

Julie nodded.

"What happened to him?" I asked.

"His father's in the Navy, and they were transferred to Houston."

"Does he know?"

"Sure he knows." She talked with her mouth full. "But he's in Houston. I'm the one who's here. I didn't have a damn thing to do with it, but I get to run to the Free Clinic and the social service place so the doctor'll get paid, then to the doctor the next day with everyone looking and wondering which one of us is pregnant—and I get to listen to her threaten to step out in front of a car every hour on the hour—" She started to take another bite, but instead she burst out, "I'm so fed up! I'm always bailing her out. All the guys love her, and she loves them all right back. So who lies for her when she wants to give one of them the brush? Who holds her head when she urps? Who holds her hand when she feels low? Me!" She cut it off suddenly and apologized. "We have lots of friends, but they all *talk*. Marcy's the only one we can trust, and Marcy's *her* friend, and she thinks I'm heartless and mean when I spout off to her! You and she are the only ones who know."

I said that was O.K., and she charged ahead, chomping and squeaking. "I know how terrible it is for her, honest, Roger. See, our parents love us and trust us and they're great, but they don't know us. They think just because she gets home by midnight and Gene stands up when Mom comes into the room that—they don't *do* anything. They haven't noticed that we are sixteen and Carmel is very sexy. I'm going to have a nervous breakdown today at two o'clock." She put down her hamburger, got out a tissue, and wiped her eyes.

"How come two o'clock?" I asked.

"Because I have an algebra exam that I'm going to flunk. It isn't fair! I'm behind in everything, and I'm not the one who's pregnant!"

"Me too," I said, "and I'm not pregnant either." Julie gave a weepy giggle. I can always make her laugh, so I went on. "Everything would be a lot less complicated if Carmel and Gene were like horny toads and got their kicks out of hugging and jumping instead of hugging and humping."

She laughed so hard that I had to pound her on the back to keep her from choking on her hamburger. She sure does appreciate my humor.

Friday, March 16

What a rotten day.

Flunked chem quiz. Then I got home from school, soaked from walking in the rain, reached in my pocket—and found an empty pocket. I flashed on my keys on top of my chest of drawers. I prowled around the house looking for an open window. It was still pouring. Pippa watched me from her house, not about to get wet unless there was something in it for her.

Of course all the windows were closed tight, not only against rain, but also against burglars since that rash of break-ins a couple months ago when Dad had the alarm system installed. I thought I got lucky when I discovered a kitchen window closed not quite square and found a wet, rusty trowel in the mud. I slid it under the sash and raised the window a quarter of an inch, which set off the alarm. I'd known it would, but I figured I could get inside quick and turn it off. No such luck. The window stuck, and nothing I could do—slipping my fingers under the sash, hammering with my fists, pushing with the heels of my hands—nothing would budge it.

I was pounding and pushing and straining when a voice croaked, "What do you think you're doing here?" I turned around, and there were our neighbors, Mr. and Mrs. North, in raincoats and rain hats, and Mr. North was pointing a big old Luger at me.

"Oh, it's you," he wheezed, and I heard the click of the safety catch, and I breathed easier.

"I forgot my key," I said.

Mr. North shouldered me aside. He looked sick. Mrs. North yammered at him, telling him the noise wouldn't kill him, but pneumonia would, to get back in the house. "He stayed home from work today because he's got a terrible flu," she told me.

He tugged and hammered and pounded the way I did, but after a few minutes he said, "I haven't got the strength. When will your family be home?"

"Vanessa'll be home in about fifteen minutes," I lied.

"Well, for fifteen minutes I won't call the cops to break into your house and turn that damn thing off, but the next time you forget your damn keys, I'm calling the cops, and I don't give a damn if they break every damn window in your damn house!" His voice got higher and higher, ending in a sneeze. He sneezed his way through the rain down the driveway and across his lawn.

"Do you want to come in and wait with us?" Mrs. North asked without enthusiasm.

"No, thank you," I said. I know my place. Definitely not with decent people who risk pneumonia on account of a creep like me. Besides, I can't stand the Norths.

I went around to the front of the house and sat on the welcome mat under the useless little overhang above the front door and tried to decide whether I am a dud, a nerd, a creep because these things happen to me, or if they happen to me because I am a dud in the first place. My father lost every key he owned last summer, but then we didn't even close our windows when we left the house, and all he had to do was climb in. Is it my fault that our block had three burglaries in six weeks, and the whole block got security systems?

A garbage truck lumbered to our curb, and a husky guy without rain gear, bearded, maybe about twenty-five, hopped out of the cab and tossed our three full thirty-five-gallon cans into the hopper as if they were basketballs, then with a flip of the wrist flung them back, empty, onto the curb. His biceps bulged, the muscles stood out on his back under his drenched T-shirt. He looked at our house with its shrieking alarm, then at me, without changing expression, activated the compactor, jumped into the cab, and guided the truck to the Norths' trash.

The Disaster Data File flipped out an item. L.A. County is running out of dumpsites. Thirty thousand tons of garbage a day and no place to put it. I sat there in the rain, the bristles of the welcome mat scratching my butt, cold, miserable, watching the trash hills soaked by the downpour grow higher and higher, covering the square city blocks, the buildings, the parks, the airport, the skyscrapers downtown, and under it all, somewhere, was good old Roger Judd the Dud.

Dad was the first to come home. He jumped out of the van, saying, "What's the matter, what's going on, what set off the alarm?"

I told him about forgetting my keys and trying to get in, but not about the Norths.

"Can't you do anything right? Can't you even hang on to a key?" he barked, pushing me aside and unlocking the front door. He turned off the alarm and closed the kitchen window easily. Then he looked at me with that familiar discouraged expression. "Roger, what are we going to do about you? When am I going to hear about something you did right for a change? It's like with your mother all over again, always disaster—"

I took a perverse comfort in his words. He never would have said such a thing in front of Lou or Vanessa. At least we were talking intimately, even if not in a friendly way.

"Yes, I know," I said bitterly. "I'm a shrimp like her, and we're both losers and downers—"

He went on. "You're going to have to straighten up and start thinking about your future. You're going to graduate next year, and I don't know what I'll be able to do for you after that. I can't—I don't know what's going to happen to Van Interior Designs. Looks like we'll have to fold up, go bankrupt—"

I stared at him. He didn't make sense. "Fold up? Why?"

He started yelling at me. "Where have you been living this last year? On Mars? In outer space? Nobody's buying cars, and that includes vans. For eight years we have more work than we can handle—now we hardly have enough work to keep Pete busy full-time!"

"Man!" I said, in a state of shock.

"I'll help you as much as I can, Roger, but I don't know what I'll be doing myself a year from now. You'll have to get yourself through college—somehow—"

Just then Vanessa came home, and he put on his happy face, and that was the end of our conversation.

Tonight Mom phoned. We went through the usual—"How are you?" "Fine." I mean, what else do you say? Give her a complete rundown on how you are flunking out of school and your father's going bankrupt, and how you spent the afternoon soaked on a scratchy welcome mat in the rain with a burglar alarm tearing your head apart? Naturally, I say, "Fine."

But tonight Mom was genuinely upbeat, not phony cheerful as usual. She got a raise, for one thing (she must be staying partly sober), she has found an apartment she loves and can afford, and she has this big surprise for me. She hasn't bought a bottle of booze since she saw me a year and a half ago. If that is true, it's really something. I never thought she could quit drinking. "Be sure to tell your father," she said. Also she is going to have another big surprise for me. She needs a little more time.

Probably going to get married, and she will want me to come to the wedding. Big deal.

Dad's beginning to crack. Yesterday he played games as usual with Vanessa and Lou, but this morning he was a bear. Came into the kitchen while I was eating breakfast out of pots at the sink after everyone else had finished. Growled why didn't I sit at the table and eat like a person. I tried to explain to him that you save three operations—taking stuff to the table, taking it off, and washing dishes—but he didn't listen.

Anyway, before I finished, Vanessa bounced in, waggling her fingers and saying, "O.K., Jack, the keys. I'm late. My appointment is in ten minutes." She and Darrell were going to this fantastic St. Patrick's Day party tonight in Bel Air, and it was such a big deal that she got a fifty-dollar perm. All week I'd been hearing how David did her this terrific favor, squeezing her in between two other jobs. She was so tense she didn't even bother to smile.

Dad looked at her as if he didn't know her. "Who said you could have my car?"

Utter disbelief on Vanessa's face. "We've been talking about it all week, Jack—"

"Have we?"

"Oh, Jack, you know the Martins are coming for dinner tonight and Mom has to shop this morning, and I should be at David's right now!"

"I mean, I'm only the guy who buys the gas," Dad went on. I couldn't believe it. It was too good to be true, only he was getting red, and I was nervous about his blood pressure. "You kids have it too damned easy. Snap your fingers and car keys fall into your lap. Snap 'em twice and you get fifty dollars for a haircut—"

Lou was poking around in the fridge, making a shopping list. She said over her shoulder, "I'm taking care of the perm, Sterling."

"That's not the point," he snarled at her. "These kids think that money is a natural phenomenon, like air and water. It's time they learned the value of a dollar!"

"If you don't want Vanessa to have the van, say so. I'll drop her off and pick her up. So dinner will be late. So the house won't be dusted. I don't give a damn!" She slammed the refrigerator door and faced him.

He actually yelled at her. "You're no help! Why don't you back me up instead of fighting me? When it comes to dealing with these kids, you're no damned good! You're like a wet sponge!"

I mean, can you believe it??!!

She yelled right back, "Count me out, buddy. Deal with them yourself!"

"I'm late!" Vanessa yelped, crying real tears. I loved it! I loved it!

"Listen, Sterling," Lou went on, giving Dad the eyeball treatment. "I'm not going to be anybody's go-between, with you on one side jumping me and Vanessa on the other. As for Roger, the less we have to do with each other, the better." (I couldn't agree more.) "What's the matter with you? You've let Vanessa have the van hundreds of times. What's wrong with you?"

"What's wrong with *me*? What's wrong with *you*? Haven't you been listening? Didn't it register when I told you we only had half a dozen jobs all month? We're facing bankruptcy, and she asks what's wrong!" He looked up at the ceiling as if wondering how anyone could be so dumb.

Lou stared at him for a second, said, "Vanessa, take my car," went over to him, and put her arms around his neck. The good old cuddle-bunny treatment.

Naturally, he melted. Took his keys out of his pocket and tossed them to Vanessa, growling, "Never mind. Here," and she ran out, bouncing fore and aft.

Lou led Dad to the chair by her kitchen desk, sat him down, anchored him by sitting on top of him. "Now, tell me about it," she said.

"I've told you. Nobody's buying. Interest rates too high— and the layoffs—so there are no vans to customize—"

Lou pulled his head to her chest, saying, "Everything will work out, honey. You're just too brilliant a man—"

Dad jerked his head away. "Who's going to pay the bills while I'm brilliantly going broke?"

"They'll always have dirty teeth, angel. We'll eat."

"The new house is out. I can't swing it now. No way."

"Maybe I can ask Frank—" Frank is Lou's first husband. He's into computers and loaded.

"*No!*"

"Just a loan to tide us over—"

"Hell, no!" Dad was heart-attack red. She dropped the subject and calmed him down by kissing him and stroking his head and asking him to tell her exactly what was happening. He started to but noticed I was still there, and he got mad all over again. Yelled at me to get off my duff and cut the front lawn. I don't see why I couldn't hear. He was my father before he was her husband. But I cleared out and cut the damned lawn.

The real point is, I can't imagine my father failing. He has never failed at anything. Like VID, for instance. He took a big chance. Gave up his good job at Aerocorp to go into partnership with Carl, designing and installing van interiors and modifying campers and like that. All the RV magazines wrote them up and carried pictures of their jobs.

Mom helped out at the office at first, but she kept making mistakes, and they fought about that on top of everything else. She was already drinking, only nobody knew but Dad and me.

But he has always made things come out his way. What happened this time?

Says I'll have to take care of myself. How? Even if someone tells me what to do, I flub it up. If no one tells me what to do—I'm lost.

Tuesday, March 20

I'd like to kill her. If I were a normal person I would know how to handle her. But I'm a creep. And she always catches me off guard. And what she says is half true.

This afternoon I was eating a sandwich in the kitchen. Vanessa bounced in, all charged up from a ride home with Darrell, humming, snapping her fingers. Pointing and bouncing at me, shooting blue sparks from her eyes, she came over, close, and said, "How can you stand it without a woman, Roger? Are you normal? Every sixteen-year-old guy I know has a woman. Except the geeks. Are you a geek, Roger?" Then her eye fell on my sandwich, and she said, "Of course not. You're a real stud. Give us half your sandwich," and she had the gall to reach for it, draping herself all over me, hanging on my shoulders, thigh to thigh, belly to back. I grabbed my sandwich and ran out of the kitchen, while she doubled over, laughing.

Instead of running away like a wimp, I should have told her to get the hell out of there, or I should have grabbed her and showed her how normal I am. Maybe that's the crux of it. Why don't I grab her? Every other guy in the world would know what to do. I know what to do. Why in the hell don't I do it?

And the way she works Dad and Lou drives me wild. Like later, while Dad and Lou were having a drink before dinner and talking about how bad times are, she came bouncing into the room and announced that she is making Scholastic Honors this year. She put on a bored pose, rubbed her fingernails over her chest. "Brains, beauty—what else is there?" Then she laughed to show how modest she is, that phony.

Dad fell for it, hook, line, and sinker. "That's what I like to hear." He gave me his Roger look—embarrassed, sour, sad.

"Come here and give us a kiss." Lou tilted her face. Vanessa kissed both Lou and Dad, then said, "—and can I go to Palm Springs Easter vacation?"

"With who?" Lou asked.

"Darrell's mom and dad are driving their motor home."

"Would you be with them?" Lou asked.

"We'd be camping real close to them. A lot of kids are going. Jennifer's going. His mom and dad'll be real near—"

"We'll see," Lou said, but the yes was already established.

And I have to beg for every little thing. Every time I want the van or a few dollars for a show.

You could say what do I expect. I don't get Scholastic Honors. I'm not sexy. I'm not much of anything.

But I'm not a phony, either.

Thursday, March 22

What am I going to do? I have screwed up worse than I ever have before in my life. Carmel will kill herself, and it will be my fault. Julie came up to me just before lunch, looking positively sick. Asked if I have a car available. I said no, what's up. She told me that Marcy, the girl who was going to drive Carmel to the abortion hospital tomorrow, got hit by a drunk who ran a light and is in the hospital herself this minute. Almost begged me to say I could get a car. I said I didn't see how. She said, "Thanks a lot, anyway," and walked away fast because she was crying.

I should have just gone my own way to the cafeteria, feeling my usual inadequate, duddish self for not helping Carmel, had lunch with that creep Marvin Mellini (I've started to pick his brains for chemistry), and let it go at that.

Instead—stupid, duddish fool—I went with Julie, sneaking behind buildings so no one would see us, past the maintenance shops. Julie, crying all the way, told me I was their last hope. Carmel has to be at the hospital in Ladera Beach by 8:30 tomorrow morning. No car. Their brother takes one to college, and their father takes the other to work. To go by bus, they have to leave their house about a quarter of six to get to the shopping center by 6:08 to catch the bus and transfer twice to be at the hospital by 7:30. The next bus connection wouldn't get them there till 8:45. Even if they could dream up a good reason for leaving the house at a quarter of six, their Pop would insist on driving them.

"So where would he drive us? To the hospital for his favorite daughter to have an abortion? He would drop dead!" Julie squeaked.

They had planned to meet Marcy at school at quarter to eight. In a car it takes half an hour, forty minutes, but it takes almost an hour and a half to go by bus.

Carmel was sitting on the ground near a trash bin, leaning against a scruffy tree, staring into space. No smile, no "hi," no sign she knew we were there. For a while no one said anything, then I suggested she change the appointment to next week, and I would reserve the van in advance. Carmel burst into tears. Julie explained that it took three weeks to get this appointment, and the doctor says it's almost too late for a simple abortion. She's getting in right under the wire.

Carmel said, "There's just no way Mom and Pop won't find out. They'll just die, they'll be so ashamed. They'll hate me."

"Come on, Carmel, they'll yell around a lot, and they'll feel bad, but they love you. You're their favorite child—"

"That's just the point. Look what I'm doing to them." Carmel got to her feet and started walking around, talking. "What am I going to do? I was scared of tomorrow, but at least I knew it would be over. *Now* what am I going to do?" She wandered out the gate in the chain-link fence.

"Where are you going?" Julie asked, following her. I went, too. I don't know if Carmel was talking to herself or Julie, but she kept up a steady stream of disjointed chatter, between sobs.

"I can't stand for Mom and Pop to know—look how I'm messing up everybody—and where is Gene? I need him—

now! I'm sorry I ever met him. It's all his fault—" She started running. "I can't face it. I don't *want* an abortion! I don't *want* to be pregnant—"

"Carmel! Wait!" Julie wailed.

"Leave me alone! Just leave me alone!" Carmel was headed for King's Highway half a block away. Headed for the heavy traffic, the way she had threatened. I knew she wouldn't stop. Maybe I was wrong, but at that time I just knew it. I put on the speed and grabbed her. Julie was right behind me. She hugged her, and they both sobbed. I knew that Carmel would try it again. I still know it. That's what's killing me. It will be my fault. I promised to get the van for tomorrow morning, and I can't.

First thing when Dad got home, as soon as he closed the door, I told him I have to have the van tomorrow all day. Vanessa flew in from the kitchen, screeching that he promised her the van for tomorrow. Didn't he remember? Lou had promised that she'd drive him to work so that she and Jennifer could do some heavy shopping at this discount place down-town right after school? Didn't he remember?

What about learning the value of a dollar? But I have more important things on my mind. I said, "Dad, it's a serious emergency."

He was already tense and frowning. "Why?" he asked.

"I have to take someone to the hospital," I told him.

Naturally, he wants to know who. I tell him it's someone he doesn't know. So far so good. I've told the truth, but when he asks me what's wrong with the guy, I start lying. I say a guy with a broken leg who's on crutches and can't take the bus has to go to the doctor.

Vanessa breaks in. "There's no one at school on crutches! It's no fair. I asked a week ago." Don't pay any attention, I tell myself. When you get involved with her, you always lose.

"What's his name?" Dad asks.

"What difference does it make?" I ask. "You wouldn't know him."

"But I would!" Vanessa butts in. "Who is it? "

Cool it, I warn myself, and I continue to look at Dad.

"What's the big secret about a broken leg? What's the kid's name?" Dad asks.

A perfectly logical way of looking at the situation. I see I have painted myself into a corner with lies. I have to admit that I was lying—with another lie.

O.K. So the guy has a venereal disease, and he doesn't want his parents to know.

That statement gives everyone a shot in the butt. Lou comes into the room holding a collander of cauliflower.

"Who is it?" Vanessa demands, trying to pin me with the Stare, but I keep my eyes on Dad, who is shaking his head. "No, I don't think I want you to get involved in this boy's problem. He can take care of himself. He isn't crippled, is he?" I should have given him a broken leg *and* a venereal disease.

"*But, Dad, I've got to!* He's going to kill himself!"

"I doubt it. I can understand that he doesn't want his parents to know, but that's his problem. He'll find a way. He'll probably be playing around again while you're still worrying about him. No, let him work it out himself."

I beg and plead with Dad, who continues to shake his head and say no and finally walks away from me. Vanessa is relaxed now. She has won again. She says, "It can't be that creep Marvin Mellini you've started hanging around with. I bet he washes his eyes every time he looks at a girl." She snickers. "Is it Marvin Mellini, Roger?"

I lose control. I shriek at her, "I don't have to clear everyone I know with your buxom bitchy highness!"

Dad grabs my arm and hustles me upstairs to my room and shoves me inside, yelling that when I'm ready to apologize to Vanessa for my language and for being rude, I can come downstairs and eat dinner.

It almost killed me, but I apologized and apologized and apologized, but no way will he give me the van.

What a screw-up. What a failure. What a freak.

What am I going to do?

SANTA BARBARA BY THE SEA BY THE SEA BY THE BEAUTIFUL SEA 11:15 A.M.!!

I did it!

I got the van!

Carmel's at the hospital right now!

I dropped them off at 8:30 on the button, tooled over to the 405, cut over to 101, zipped along past Malibu and Oxnard and Ventura and the Six Mile Beaches listening to the Black Dawn doing "Looking for My Love" and "Bitter Brew" about fifty times until I figured I ought to stop at Santa Barbara because I don't have a credit card with me for gas. So here I am, parked by the beach, writing this down in my school spiral which I'll tear out and clip to my journal.

Because, I mean, this I gotta keep and remember from here on out, forever and ever.

So what happened? Let me tell you, baby. *Let me tell you!!*

I hardly slept at all last night. Lou had an early appointment, so she and Dad left early. Look at how he puts himself out for that slime. I went downstairs, and there was her slimy highness sitting at the table drinking orange juice out of one of Lou's crystal wine glasses. A soup bowl full of cereal, and coffee in a cup and saucer from the good china, were in front of her. She treats herself like royalty. The sight of her stuffing her face, those things pointing out ahead of her like a couple of guns, enraged me. I jumped over to her chair and stood over her, hands clenched, heart pounding. I snarled,

"Vanessa, I've got to have that van!"

She didn't even look up. "No way," she said.

"*Please!*" I begged. "God, Vanessa, wouldn't you help a friend? Suppose it was Darrell or Jennifer?"

She finished eating. She got up, gathering the dishes carefully. She said to me, "You don't know anyone with any venereal disease. You don't know anyone, period. You know you're lying, and I know you're lying, so why don't you level with me? Why do you want the van?" Those flat blue irises fix me with the Stare.

"Please, Vanessa. I gotta take someone for an abortion."

In slow motion those big blue eyes open wider and wider. Her eyebrows go up and up. Her jaw drops. The dishes in her hand crash to the floor.

"*You what?*"

I had been about to explain that I didn't do it, but as I watch Vanessa's universe come unglued—planets shooting out of their orbits, the sun wobbling all over the sky, cuckoo birds warbling in her head—I change my mind. "See why I couldn't tell?" I say. "Do you want it to be on your conscience that she kills herself?" Then, to bring her out of her trance, I point to the dishes. "You broke the good china. You're going to catch hell."

She drops to her knees, making little moaning noises. She picks up a few pieces, then sits back on her heels, staring up at me.

"You—??!! *But when?* You're always home! Or at that dumb field—*the field*," she repeats, a great dawning in her eyes. "Who is it? You better tell me. I'll find out!"

The bullying tone and the Stare retorch my fury. I become

a red-eyed monster with arms like tree trunks and fangs longer than my chin. I am strong! and I am *mean*! I grab her by the hair and lean over her, nose to nose.

"If you say one word, *one word*, to anyone, I'll kill you!" I hiss at her.

The blue eyes widen with fear and surprise. She tries to jerk away from me, queeping, "What do you think I am, some kind of fink?" I tighten my grip and give an extra yank for all the times I've wanted to kill her. "Roger, you're hurting me!"

With a final tug, I let go, saying, "I mean it!"

She goes back to picking up the shattered china and crystal, mumbling, "Look what you made me do! Mama'll kill me!" As she drops the broken dishes in a paper bag, she shrieks at me, "Shrimp! Creep! I'll find out! You wait! I'll find out! I'll fix you!"

She will, too.

I went upstairs to get my books. When I came down, she was on the phone, finishing a conversation with Darrell. "Darrell is going to work you over," she yelled at me. "Creep! Shrimp! Sneak!"

"If it happened to her, it could happen to you, baby," I told her. "Take care. "

I had the joy of seeing those big blue eyes fill with worry. I'm not afraid of Darrell. He's too practical, too political to lay hands on me. Blackmail is more his style. He and Vanessa will spy on me. Or plain rat out. I'll just never let them find out who it is.

I was a few minutes late, and Carmel and Julie were stiff with panic. I could tell from half a block away the way they hugged their books and looked at every car. They piled into the back of the van and sat together in one lounge chair. Carmel chewed her nails and worried that something would go wrong and she wouldn't be out of the hospital this afternoon, and Julie kept reassuring her that everything will be all right. When we got to the hospital entrance, Carmel grabbed Julie's hand and said, "Oh, Julie, I'm so scared. Is this really me? What am I doing here?" Julie hugged her and comforted her and kind of pulled her out of the van. I watched them go into the hospital. It was sad.

But anyway, I got them there on time. Then buzzed on up here. Found this parking place. Couldn't sit still. Ran along the surf for a mile or so. Man, it is grand! Sky blue, air clean, three- or four-foot breakers, guys surfing. Hard to believe that the planet is in danger of suffocating from its own pollution. When you look out over the Pacific and realize that two-thirds of the earth is good, clean water, you wonder if maybe those environmental dudes are making a mistake.

I'm starving. Only had a dollar and a half in my pocket. When I got off the freeway, stopped and had a 99¢ breakfast and a candy bar, but I'm still hungry. It's 12:30. I'm going to start back. Better allow too much time than not enough.

10:30

Just clipped the other page to this journal. End of a perfect day. Everyone has gone somewhere—Dad and Lou to a show, Vanessa and Darrell to The Purple Jupiter. She is supposed to be grounded for a week because she broke the dishes, but it begins tomorrow because Darrell already had tickets. I surprised everybody by being polite to her. Dad is pleased.

Thinks maybe I am turning around. She looked at me as if she would throw up.

Anyway, at three-thirty I was at the hospital. Drove them home. Carmel was pale and tired, but O.K. When I helped her out of the lounge chair in the van, she kissed my ear and told me she would never forget what I did for her, that she did not know what she would have done without me. I told her that was O.K. and helped her out of the van. She leaned on Julie, and I followed, carrying their books.

Julie opened the door. Her father was watching TV. She said, "Hi, Pops, how come you're home? I think Carmel had a relapse. She feels terrible. Roger drove us home. Papa, this is Roger Judd."

He's bald, paunchy, and drinking a beer. He got up, and we shook hands while he answered Julie's question. "No business. Between the rain this winter and the so-called recession nobody's buying tires. Al can handle it by himself today."

Mrs. Bierre came in, wiping floury hands on a paper towel.

"My God! What's this? What's wrong? Carmel, what is it?" She squeaks like Julie.

"Oh, Ma, take it easy. I think she had a relapse. She was throwing up at school," Julie said.

"I told you you got up too soon! I told you—" Mrs. Bierre squeaked.

"Oh, Ma, I'll be all right tomorrow," Carmel said.

"You get into bed and stay there, and I mean it!" Carmel left the room, and Mrs. Bierre said in a normal voice, "She'll be all right. A good sleep is the best medicine. And vitamins. She ran herself down. She's grieving over Gene. You know Gene?" she asked me. "Such a nice boy. And my kids take things so serious, too serious, that's my nature, too—"

"Hey, Grace, come up for air," Mr. Bierre broke in. Then he asked me, "How about a beer?"

"You shouldn't offer him beer! He's not of age!" Mrs. B. squeaked.

Mr. B. winked at me. "Do him good. He needs to be filled out. Put hair on his chest," he said.

I got a kick out of both of them, but I knew too much to be comfortable, so I said I'd take a raincheck. Mrs. Bierre beamed at me. I know she said I was a nice boy after I left. She thanked me for driving her girls home and invited me to come again. Julie walked me to the door and radiated me with a ten-thousand watter. She's a good-looking chick herself. Sensational bod. Sensational as Carmel's. That family is about 180 degrees different from Mom and Dad and Lou and Vanessa. They are like their house—kind of funky and old-fashioned and comfortable.

But look at Carmel.

Man, am I bushed. All of a sudden. Totally. After all, I didn't sleep last night. I'm just unwinding. I think I'm unwound.

Good night, Roger Judd, the Un-Dudded.

For once I know what it means to be on top of the world. I won! I got the best of Vanessa. I got Carmel to the hospital and home. Roger Judd the Dud did not screw up!

I knew I'd meet Julie today when I took Pippa to the field. She was waiting for me, I think. She sort of appeared out of the eucalyptus trees near Maple. We started walking, and I asked how Carmel was, and she said fine. Said their mom made her stay in bed. I sort of expected a personal message from Carmel, but Julie just kept repeating that they didn't know how they could thank me for what I had done, so I got the message. No message from Carmel.

Julie and I had a ball reliving yesterday. Julie said once Carmel was in the hospital, she was very calm, and everything moved along the way it was supposed to. But Julie was so nervous waiting, *she* threw up when she tried to eat lunch. I told her about being afraid I wouldn't get the van, and how I didn't sleep all Thursday night. She groaned and asked what was the problem, and I told her the daughter of the woman my father married had it reserved.

"I didn't know you had a stepsister. I don't know anything about you. Does she go to Central?" she asked.

When I said yeah, everybody knows Vanessa McCloskey, she said, "Oh, her. No offense, but I can't stand her. She's always putting on a big act."

I laughed and said, "No offense to me. I live with her."

Then Julie wanted to know how I did get the car, so I told

her how Vanessa thinks I got someone pregnant, and how she was so zonked she dropped the good dishes because she considers me a creep who couldn't get a woman, let alone get her pregnant, and how she's burning because she doesn't know who the girl is. Julie and I had a million laughs. We agreed not to have anything to do with each other at school because of the VFBI—Vanessa Fink Bureau of Investigation. Julie will warn Carmel.

We circled the field, the dogs coming and going as usual. We crossed the railroad tracks and climbed the north side of the cut to the high portion of the field, and what did we see, across on the south road by the toad pond, but Darrell's white Corona. It was stuck in the mud up to the hub caps in the gunk on the side of the road. He would have been smarter to go slow through the middle of the puddle.

He and Vanessa were having a conference at the rear of the car. They peered into the puddle, then they picked their way to the front of the car. They had another conference, then picked their way to the back of the car again. They went back and forth like this for about twenty minutes, sometimes trying to slide rocks under the wheels.

Then Vanessa looked at her watch. I told Julie that she is grounded for a week, not supposed to see Darrell except at school, but that Lou and my father were playing tennis, so she and Darrell sneaked out to spy on me. It was twenty of four, and my father and Lou were due back around four. Darrell reached in from the passenger's side to get his keys, and he and Vanessa started back toward Maple. We could tell from the way they lifted their feet that they had a couple pounds of mud on each shoe.

"He's going to have to get a tow," I told Julie.

"What a shame," she said, giving me a ten-thousand watter.

It's midnight. Have been watching old movies, but not really seeing them, mostly thinking about my fantastic two days.

But tomorrow without fail I'm digging into chemistry and English.

Tuesday, March 27

Carmel is back. She looks terrible. I am under surveillance by the VFBI. Vanessa and her buddies watch me from behind doors, lockers, across the cafeteria. I can spot them every time. I just go on my duddish way as usual, hanging out with fellow creep Marvin Mellini. He is very sharp in chemistry, so I'm trying to butter him up. I can hardly keep from asking Darrell how much the tow set him back. What a crack-up.

Cut out after third period and walked all over Del Amo. What brilliant administrator dreamed up the idea of taking roll in third period for all day and just spot-checking the other classes? Very convenient for goof-offs. I've been too high since Friday to sit in class. It's too depressing to face how far behind I am in everything. Let me enjoy the fruits of victory a little while longer. Next week I'll settle down for sure. Then Easter vacation is the week after, and I'll work like a dog. I was almost caught up before the abortion.

Thursday, March 29

Blew it again. After a week of living like a normal human being and beginning to think there was hope for me. Today was superfine—until she gave me the poppy. Creep! Nerd! Wimp! She *knows* what a dud I am now. Not that she'll talk— she's no Vanessa—*but she knows*.

Met Julie in the field. Asked why Carmel looks so bad. J. told me that C. is full of guilt for having had an abortion. I said, hey, the reason I stuck my neck out for her was because I was afraid she'd throw herself in front of a truck if she *didn't* have the abortion. Julie said yes, but now Carmel is thinking about what she did to the baby. I hadn't thought about the baby. That's a pretty heavy load. What a lot of grief and trouble this whole deal has been. And to make matters worse, Carmel has not heard from Gene for a week and a half, and he knew about the abortion. I told Julie I couldn't understand why Carmel still likes him after the way he treated her.

"She's in love," Julie said. She gave me a quick glance. "Have you ever been in love, Roger?"

She must be blind or dumb or something, but now she knows. Who would want to go and fall in love with me?

I didn't answer, and we didn't talk about Carmel any more. It was a beautiful day today. No smog. Clear enough to see the mountains, and they must be at least forty miles away. The sky was blue, and Julie said the weeds dripped sunshine when they waved in the breeze. I saw exactly what she meant.

We cut through them to where an oil pump was groaning and squeaking and clanking inside its chain-link square. She hooked her fingers through the fence and pressed against it, babbling how the pumps remind her of Moslems praying, bowing, only Moslems aren't named Lufkin, which is painted in black and white on the shafts of most of them. I didn't pay much attention to what she was saying. I was watching her breasts squeeze flat against the chain-link and pop back into shape when she moved away. She rocked back and forth a number of times, squashing and popping. She has a fantastic bod, just as fantastic as Carmel's. It's just her nose that kind of spreads. The rest of her is sensational, but man, what a motor mouth.

We got back to the road, and she saw her footprints in the dust. "Footprints! I exist!" she squeaked. I asked her what she was talking about. "I see my footprints, so I know I exist," she told me.

"Is that what it takes to convince you?" I snickered. "I can see you. Will you take my word for it?"

"I might be a figment of your imagination, except that figments don't weigh anything, and it takes weight to make footprints."

I looked hard at the road. "What footprints?" I said with a straight face.

She looked down at the road. "My God!" she said. "I don't see yours, either. We're a couple of figments!"

We sort of floated over the ground, moaning and waving our arms like ghosts—the way you played when you were a kid. Then we just walked while Pippa and Butchie checked for underground movements—gophers, mice, whatever. Julie knows all the different kinds of birds, I mean the little ones that look alike. She showed me wildflowers. I never noticed before that there are sprinklings of wildflowers among the weeds. Lupines and owl's clover and I forget the others she showed me.

She picked a poppy and said, "Look, your eyes can feel how silky smooth the petals are just by looking." She passed it over her eyelids and cheeks and lips, then held it out to me.

"Here is a piece of the sunset sky—to—thank you for everything—"

I took it, looking into the deep, dark shine of her eyes, at her lips, the base of her throat, her breasts (the little darlings!), the curve of her hips—then I blew it. I said, "Thank you," like a schoolteacher, and started back for Maple as if the devil were on my tail. Julie could hardly keep up with me. We didn't say another word, except good-bye. She wanted me to kiss her. Everybody kisses. Big deal. Why the panic? She's not Vanessa. What's wrong with me?

All I have been able to think about since I left her is how I want to kiss her. She's so lovely. But she's probably given up on me. Probably thinks I don't like her. Probably thinks I don't go in for that sort of thing. Probably thinks I'm weird. I am. And tragic. I'll probably die without loving a woman.

Dear Mom and Dad,

I am sorry you will get a shock at what I'm going to do. But I think after you get over it you will be better off.

This book will explain.

Good luck.

Roger

Well, I'm still here. This journal was on my desk, open to the suicide note. I was just getting up on the chair when Vanessa knocked at the door. I guess it's lucky for Carmel that she did. I didn't even think about everybody reading all about her and Gene and the abortion.

And—God!—everybody would have known about me and Julie!

I knew something was up yesterday when I came home from the field with Pippa. Dad was already home, waiting for me. Said he wanted to see me in the living room, and he closed both doors. Started out smooth. Said he received some interesting mail from Central High School, and I began to shake. With good reason. One communication informed him that I was flunking English and chemistry. The letter from the Attendance Office informed him that I have been absent from afternoon classes fourteen times this semester without excuses.

"Where were you?" he asked. The veins in his temples stood out like cords. I told him I can make up the F's, that I'm actually borderline.

He cut loose. "Where the hell have you been going?" he roared, and I could see his blood pressure shoot up. "I know you've been taking the car away from Vanessa!"

"That rotten fink!" I yelled.

He grabbed me by the shoulders and shook me. "Where

have you been going with that car?" His eyes were so cold, man.

"I only took it one day!" I said, but I could see he didn't believe me, which drove me wild. "Did she say I took it more than that Friday? If she did, she's a liar! You always believe her! Why don't you believe me?"

He yelled at me to keep my voice down, but I kept on yelling. I couldn't help it. I told him he acts as if she's perfect, and he yelled that that was a lot of nonsense. He said she's just a lot easier to live with than someone who sulks and whines and looks like a bum.

"She gets Scholastic Honors!" he said. "What comes from you? Nothing but bad news! Don't you think it tears me up that Lou is so proud of her, and I have to make excuses for you? 'Wait till he finds himself,'" he mimicked, the veins in his temples about to bust.

"You're ashamed of me! Why don't you be honest? I don't belong in this lousy love nest!" I yelled.

He slapped me hard. Both sides of my face. Yelled that he doesn't have to take this crap from me, and he's not going to. And I am going to tell him where I go with the car if he has to beat it out of me.

I cringed, but said nothing. I was fighting to keep from bawling like a kid. He yanked me to my feet by my jacket and stuck his fist in my face. "Roger—" was all he said, but his face was so bloodless and dead I was afraid he was having a heart attack right then, even though his hold on me was like iron. It would be my fault. I couldn't let him die.

So I said, "I had to take a girl for an abortion."

His eyes went cuckoo like Vanessa's, and he let go of me

so abruptly that I fell backward against the end table, knocking it over and breaking the lamp on it with a loud crash. From the floor I watched his eyes come back into focus much faster than Vanessa's. A light went on.

"Now we're getting somewhere. You sure fooled me, I must say. You don't look—I didn't think you were—ready—you sure had me fooled—"

"I didn't do it," I said, brokenhearted at having to disappoint my father. But he didn't believe me.

"Is the girl all right?" I nod. "Good. Who is it?" I shake my head. "Now, listen, Roger, you're going to tell me so I can get everything straightened out."

"But I didn't do it, Dad!"

"Then why did you take her for the abortion?"

I told him the whole story except for names.

"Do her parents think you did it?" he asked.

"No. They don't even know she was pregnant."

"So what did you get out of it?" he asked, looking at me skeptically.

"I told you. I was afraid she'd kill herself."

His glance wavered. His color was getting better, but he was still breathing hard. "Are you sure you and she didn't get together? You can tell me. It isn't the first time—you aren't the only one who ever—I can understand—"

"I didn't do it," I tell him again. "Vanessa thinks I did, but I didn't. Dad, don't tell her I didn't," I beg.

He blows up again. "What the hell do you mean by that? Why would she think you did if you didn't? Are you trying to give me another cock-and-bull story like the kid with venereal disease?"

Just then Lou knocks loudly, then timidly opens the door.

She takes in the overturned table and the broken lamp. She is scared. Her voice shakes as she says, "Carole is on the phone. She wants to speak with Roger."

Dad goes off like an H bomb, yelling, "That's exactly what we need right now, a dim-witted chat with your brilliant mother!" Lou scurries away. "Answer the phone!" he roars at me, and I go to the phone and go through the old routine. "How are you?" she asks from New York. "Fine," I tell her from California. I mean, what else do you say?

She's bubbling about her big surprise. She's got enough booze money saved to buy me a cheap plane ticket to come to New York for a month this summer. Every time she wanted a drink, she'd put the money in some kind of vase, then take it to the bank. She gets a week off, and we'll take a couple little trips, and when she works I can explore New York by myself. Then she asks to talk to my father. She's pretty proud of herself, and she tells me to stay on the line and listen to her brag.

So I call him and go upstairs to the extension in their bedroom, but all the way I hear him yelling out the juicy details of my flunking out and taking a girl for an abortion, and when I get on the line again, she says, "Roger?" in this dead voice, all the bubble and fun out of it.

Then he begins to yell again. It's her turn now. He's sending me to her. Let *her* find out what my problem is. He's had it. She's yelling he can't do this to her. She has made plans to have me this summer, not now. And he yells, let her find out what it's like to live with a hostile, sulky sixteen-year-old who can't do anything right. He's tried and failed. It's up to her now.

And she says he always does this to her, always the way

he wants it, always wrecking her plans. Then she remembers I'm on the line. Tries to calm down. Says we'll talk again and work things out when everybody's calmer. She'll call tomorrow. Her voice is shaking. Probably ran out and got a bottle as soon as she hung up.

So this is what comes of winning out over Vanessa and helping Carmel. Even when I win I lose.

I didn't leave my room all night. Where would I go? There is no place on earth where I belong. When the chips are down, neither of them has a place for me. But what gets me is how can he forget? How he held me after she left and even let me sleep against him when I couldn't fall asleep by myself? And I remember, when he went out on dates, how I never fell asleep until I heard the front door close and him talking to the sitter and I knew he was safe. And the good times we had together. What about that Colorado River trip? And her. She just went away. I had my own home, with Mom and Dad, my own block, my own school, my own friends. Then I had nothing but Dad and a TV.

I am so totally fed up with falling between the cracks of other people's lives.

I was thinking all that when I wrote the note. I left this journal open at that page. Then I slung my belt over that high clothes bar in the closet that her father put up for Vanessa's million extra clothes when this was her room. I had everything ready and I was standing on the chair just about to slip the belt over my head and jump. I remembered Julie's words that the saddest thing in the world is to die young, and I cried. Man, you don't know how all alone you are till you stand on a chair about to jump and you know that this is all there is. No afterwards. Done. Finished. Good-bye.

There is this soft knock at the door, and Vanessa's voice, talking fast and low. "Roger, I swear to God they made me tell. I didn't want to, but he kept yelling at me—" That phony liar.

I get so mad, man! I jump off the chair and throw my shoes at the door, calling her a yellow, rotten fink, a liar, a fraud, a buxom bitch. Things like that. The shoes hit the door with big echoing *vrooms* like cannon. When I run out of shoes, I send my jar of shoe cream after them. My clock flies through the air and kills itself. I watch me hurl whatever I can lay my hands on, listen to me yell names I never knew I knew. There go my radio, my bed pillows, my lamp, my books, the old Snoopy bookends. Man, the airspace in my room was busier than LAX.

My father is pounding on the door, rattling the knob, yelling for me to open up. I keep throwing things and cussing until he tells Lou to go for the hatchet. Anyway, I had run out of stuff to throw, so I open the door a few inches. We face each other, both of us pale and panting. Over his shoulder I see Lou crying. A slice of light on the hall carpet tells me that Vanessa's door is open.

He grabs me by the shoulders and tries to shake me, but he doesn't have it any more. Tells me he's ashamed of me acting like a hysterical fool, and by God I am going to apologize to Vanessa.

"She should apologize to you for all the times she stands behind you and mimics you and then kisses you when she gets what she wants!" I bawl.

"I do not!" she screeches from her room.

"Why am I the liar? She lied about the car. She knows I only took it that one time, but she lied! Ask her! What other time did I take it? Ask her the date!" Lou and Dad are staring at her, waiting for her answer.

"Leave me alone!" she screams, and slams her door.

Dad lets go of me. He slumps and says, "I can't take any more." He looks around my room kind of dazed. "Clean up this mess tomorrow." He gives me a sharp look as if an idea suddenly struck him. "You all right?"

I turn away from him, sick. What a dumb, stupid question.

It's taken me all day to get this down. Write a little, sleep a little. Cry. I don't leave my room except to go to the can. Lou and Vanessa are home. Too broken up by the act Dad and I put on. They have been fighting, too. I heard Lou tell Vanessa she had gone too far, that she was spoiled and had never learned to give in any give-and-take. But when Lou brought my lunch, she tried to put the blame on me. Said she wished I had come to her about my feelings about Vanessa. Said I take Vanessa too seriously, that she's a child who's full of fun. That made me laugh, which teed her off.

"She is *not* mean, Roger. She's a good kid. You don't understand her."

That was when I walked out on her and went to the can. Just now she came back for the lunch dishes. Her eyes were red and puffy. She said in a wavery voice, "Roger, I wish you didn't hate us so much." She was standing against the door, so I went to the window and turned my back on her.

She began to cry. "I'm crazy about your father. Roger, give me a break."

Give *her* a break. Now ain't that a laugh!

I was in bed. I was just reaching to turn out my lamp, because I was really bushed, but now I'm all stirred up again and awake. Dad just came into my room. Looked around. Said, "You cleaned up the mess. I see the lamp still works."

"No, it's the other one, the twin," I told him.

"We were hell on lamps yesterday, you and I. What about the clock and the radio?"

"Broken."

His wrinkles deepened. "Look at this door." He meant the dents I put in it. The raw wood shows in some spots. But I didn't look at it or at him. I kept my eyes on the window while he went on. By his voice I could tell he was keeping hold of himself.

"Now, this is what's going to happen. I just talked to your mother. You're going to New York Saturday. I made a return reservation for Easter Sunday. You and she might hit it off so well you'd rather be with her. Maybe she'll understand you. If that's so, you can go for good this summer." His voice was rough but not loud, but as he went on, it kept going up and up. "But you're not going to throw away this whole year of school. You're coming back after Easter, and you're going to hit those books. If you need a tutor, you'll have, by God, a tutor. And you'll go to every single class every single day. As long as you live with me this is the way it's going to be. Got it? Answer me!" I nodded. "O.K. I made appointments with your English and chemistry teachers and the vice-principal tomorrow at noon."

That's good old Sterling Judd. On the ball. Get things fixed up. Chop chop.

We looked at each other. He seemed to be on the verge of coming to me. I was ready to throw myself at him and hug him like I used to, but all he did was clear his throat and kind of stammer, "Let's consider this a clean break. It'll be better if you clear out of here—we'll all cool off and do some thinking and see what we come up with."

I turned my back on him, and he left. This is the second time I've heard my father stammer. He really is kicking me out. He really wants me to clear out.

I wish Vanessa had waited five minutes before she knocked. I would be dead. They would have found me this morning, and by now I'd be in a box somewhere. Like a pair of socks. Or like the gopher. Both of us heroes, both of us losers.

Wednesday, April 4

We had our conferences with Baker and Fretter and Dr. Prinque. After Easter I'm going to have a chem major from UCLA to tutor me. If I make two extra book reports to take the place of my incomplete journal and keep up my grades, I'll be O.K. in English.

Dad and the Prinque didn't hit it off. The Prinque tried to one-up my father, and you just don't do that to Sterling Judd. P. started out smooth, with the cordial handshake and soft voice. Told Dad sadly that I have enough unexcused absences to be sent up before a juvenile judge. Dad bristled right away. Told the Prinque he came to get things straightened out, not to be threatened. The Prinque said he was not threatening, just giving him the facts. Dad said I am no street trash J.D., and the Prinque said he didn't say I was, but here are the absences. Holds out the roll books. Dad says he knows about the absences, that's why he took valuable time to come here. And the Prinque says he quite understands. Many parents take their valuable time only when the student is already in severe difficulty. And Dad says he can't understand how this situation was allowed to develop for so long. And the Prinque says he can't understand how parents can be so completely unaware of how their children spend their time. Wasn't he interested in what I was learning in the classroom—and outside?

And I sit like a totem pole with my face hanging out while they agree in complete hostility—no more cuts.

Afterwards Dad and I went to lunch. He spent the first fifteen minutes cussing out the Prinque. Then, after the waitress brought us our stuff, he asked me to tell him in plain English about the pregnancy. So I told him the whole story. He asked me for the second time what I got out of it, and again I told him I was afraid Carmel would kill herself.

"Aren't there agencies to handle that kind of thing—hot lines, clinics—"

"She'd already been to the Free Clinic, and there wasn't time. She had the appointment for the next day, and it would have been too late before she could make another one."

"You sure you didn't have anything to do with her—nothing at all?" I shook my head in shame. "What's all this about not telling Vanessa?" He looked straight into me.

It came to me in a flash that I had asked him not to tell Vanessa, and he hadn't. I wanted to thank him. Again I had this sense of failing him. Not that I want to be a father at this point, but he would have understood, and I would not have to let him see what a wimp, what a washout I am in my relationship with Vanessa. It's like tearing my gut to let him know how she's always rubbing against me and giggling and asking me if I'm normal, and how I can't handle it and usually run away.

But this information sent *his* sun wobbling all over the sky. He stared at me with his mouth open, full of food.

"You still don't believe me about her, do you?" I said bitterly.

He looked into his plate and fidgeted. "This is a shock to me—I can't believe — Of course I'll be watching—" Then he looked at me. "But your main problem is you, Roger,

Vanessa or no Vanessa. Listen, you're sixteen years old. You can't sulk your life away. You're going to have to shape up. You have to get out and live!"

"Sure, but how? What shall I do?"

"Get a job! Make friends! What do other kids do?"

"The hell with the other kids!" I was suddenly furious. "I'm *me*! What should *I* do? How do *I* start?"

He sort of collapsed, tired, bushed. "You have to find that out for yourself."

We didn't talk after that. When we finished lunch, we shopped for some dress pants that were long enough and some shirts and things. He kept complaining that I'm costing him an arm and a leg just when he can least afford it. On top of everything else. No wonder he wants to get rid of me. Picked up plane ticket. Saturday morning, 10:45. I've never flown before. Hope I don't puke.

This morning I was tunneling through the noise in the hall, not letting it touch me, when this high, piping squeak at my elbow got through to me. Julie. "Were you sick?" she asked.

I told her my father found out. She stopped dead still. I revived her by telling her nobody knows it was Carmel. "I gotta go," she said. "Meet us by the trash bins at lunch." She darted away.

She and Carmel were waiting for me. We all had take-out from the cafeteria. We ate while I told them the whole story, including that my father is sending me to my mom in New York Saturday.

"Forever?" Julie squeaked. I said no, just for Easter week for now, but maybe for good later.

She turned on Carmel. "Look at the mess you got him into!" she yelled.

Carmel started crying. She didn't even have a tissue to blow her nose with. Julie had to give her one. And I used to think she was so great and Julie was such a nit. The only things Carmel has going for her actually are her bod and her nose, but Julie is smarter and has a sense of humor, and actually her nose isn't all that bad.

Lou just came in. She's totally herself again — big bright blue eyes and all. Said, "I'm not going to disappear, Roger, so we might as well try to get along. I told Vanessa, and I'm telling you, I'm not going to let you kids wreck my life." She put a box on my dresser and left. It's a tote bag for the plane. The cute little barfy bon voyage card was signed, "Love, Vanessa and Lou."

Ready and packed.

It has been a weird day and evening. Waiting for—what? I can tell that Dad feels bad by the way he looks at me. So do I. I wish I knew how to do things right.

One accomplishment—I queered the Palm Springs deal for Vanessa. She is going to stay with her grandparents in Lawndale for Easter week so Dad and Lou can have some time alone to sort things out. What a pleasant house guest she's going to be!

Today in English Carmel slid a paperback book on the arm of my chair as she walked past. There was an envelope sticking out. It held a bon voyage card. On the side opposite the message there were two notes.

Dear Roger,

I am sorry for the trouble I caused you. You'll never know what you did for me. You saved my life, and look at the mess I got you into. I told G. about everything. He phoned last night. He had been sick. Says to say hi. Have a nice trip.

Sincerely,

C.

The second one said,

Dear Roger—

I wish we could do something great for you, like buy you a gold watch or a gold Porsche or a gold world, but we're flat broke. You can read this on the plane and take your mind off the fact that there's nothing under you but thirty thousand feet of thin air.

I sure hope everything works out.

You know why the initials—the VFBI.

Yours *very* truly,

J.

The book is called *The Treason Trust*. Spy crap.

It's definitely getting light. D-Day. Zero hour, minus five or six hours. I didn't sleep much. Couldn't stop thinking about him kicking me out and Mom not knowing me and me not knowing her and how I'm contributing to the rape of the planet flying in an aircraft spewing hydrocarbons into the atmosphere. If it doesn't crash. Four nights ago I was about to hang myself. Now I'm worried about my plane crashing. Doesn't make sense.

Got up and repacked everything and took another shower. He made me get a haircut yesterday. Took me to where he gets his styled. Whenever I see myself in the bathroom mirror, I almost say, "Pardon me," and split.

Have checked the tote and my wallet. Have ticket. He gave me ten brand-new tens last night to take Mom to dinner and a show. Said if he knows her, she'll be broke. She never could manage money or anything else. I just hope she stays sober.

I think I'll change into my new slacks and a long-sleeved shirt.

Is it only two hours since we were standing around near the boarding gate, bouncing glances off each other? Man, I felt like a cat about to be thrown out of a car. Finally I mumbled that I guessed I would go, and they all looked relieved. Dad shook my hand, squeezed my shoulder, told me to have a good trip. Lou kissed me and wished me the best of luck. Then—can you believe it?—Vanessa puckered up and stuck her face at me! I just said good-bye and turned my back on her and left. Dad called me, and I stopped without turning around, waiting for the order to apologize. But it didn't come. Instead, he spun me around and hugged me the way he used to. Growled, "Take care of yourself," breathing hard, and we walked away from each other. I was thinking, If you're so broken up, why are you sending me away from you?

So I got on the plane and squeezed down the aisle with the other passengers and took my seat by the window in front of the wing. I stared at the big jet in the next bay with the hose in its belly and all the runabouts and trucks and ground crews so no one would see how bad I felt.

A metallic voice over the intercom jarred me out of my misery, telling us how to use our oxygen masks and the seat cushions as a flotation device in case we went down in the Pacific. Then the captain's voice welcomed us, gave us the altitude and route, and commanded us to fasten seat belts. I buckled up and went into my totem pole act while we waited our turn to take off.

Without warning our engines opened up full throttle, and we glided over the tarmac, gathering speed, rushing, rushing! rushing! faster! faster! until we were hurtling! The ground dropped, and buildings and trees and streets shrank under my eyes. Tipped back against my seat, I felt the ascent in my gut—like riding a rocket!

We're over the Pacific, pointed at the sky. Way, way below, the coastline curves around the stubby Palos Verdes Penin-sula, and across the channel Catalina floats on a million sparkles. But there is space! The peninsula and the island and the coastline are insignificant in the blue-black ocean. And the blue-black ocean is smaller than the blue-gold sky!

We level off, dip a wing, and turn slowly back toward land. Now we are over wall-to-wall people, their little squares stretching in all directions, slashed by a few river channels and the freeways, which tie it all together. We fly parallel to the mountains, huge barriers that keep the wall-to-wall people from spilling over into the desert. From ground level they are either invisible or dark, smoggy shapes, but I can see snow-shining peaks, sun-drenched ridges, blue valleys—

Look, Ma, I'm flying!

Have been to the can like an experienced traveler. Checked out this old crate. Super. Glad Dad got me a window seat where I can see everything. Right now we are over a red desert with a pattern of erosion that looks like the flames of hell.

Just ate my steak and peas, watching how slowly we move at six hundred and fifty miles per hour.

Forty minutes till Kennedy. We have been over cloud cover since Kansas. Tried to read *The Treason Trust* but can't get interested. I am not looking forward to being with Mom. Being with her is an awful drag. I hope she isn't drinking heavily. I can't believe she hasn't had a drink in a year and a half. She managed to stay dry for a week every summer— but a year and a half? I hardly know her. A week every summer—except last summer—doesn't promote intimacy. I wish this flight were just beginning. I wish it would never end. I wish I could always be between takeoff and landing.

Sunday, April 8

I am waiting for the call from Dad. Mom went out to get deli for supper and do some grocery shopping.

What a freak-out of a day! Not that we did so much, just walked around Brooklyn Heights, but we had a lot of laughs. Mom blows my mind! She is so totally different now. At the airport I almost didn't recognize her. I was looking for this mousy, messy, out-of-it female, and I see this sharp-looking person standing alone—short hair, dressed very New York, big blue eyes searching the debarking passengers—and by the time I realized that this was Mom, she had spotted me, and we ran to each other and hugged. Also she is little! I tower over her. And she kept saying, "You're so big, Roger, I didn't recognize you. And you got your hair styled! And you're handsome!"

"You're sharp yourself, Mom," I said. "You're a knock-out!"

She liked that. Told me proudly she's been dry for twenty-one months—since the last time she was in Del Amo. Must be so—she's so different. She really was glad to see me. I could tell. All the way to the bus she squeezed my arm and kept saying, "Oh, Roger, baby, you're here! You're really here!" If I had been smaller she would have kept on kissing me.

On the bus she asked about my flight, and I told her all about how neat it was. Then we had to transfer to a subway. She asked about Dad and VID. I said he might go bankrupt.

She was shocked. Like me, she couldn't believe he could fail. "He put his life's blood into that damned business. For his sake and yours, I hope he doesn't."

She looked out the bus window for a while, then asked for details. I answered her as well as I could until we went underground and couldn't talk. We went clattering and squealing through this black, endless tunnel, whipping past a lighted cavern every so often. We got off in one of them, onto a high concrete platform between two sets of tracks and rode an elevator up to a shabby arcade of an old, unused hotel. There is positively nothing that old in the entire city of Del Amo. We walked about eight blocks to her apartment through Brooklyn—old big square buildings like downtown Los Angeles. I was thinking more of the cold. My teeth were chattering.

"Haven't you guys heard of spring?" I asked Mom.

"It's not that cold. Your blood is thin," Mom said, squeezing my arm. I noticed, though, that the trees are still bare. Maybe their sap is thin. But she went on chattering, asking how Dad and Lou are getting along. When I told her like a couple of lovebirds, she pressed her lips together and got deep wrinkles between her eyes. She went up in smoke when I told her that Dad gave me a hundred bucks for us to have a good time.

"He can take his money—" she brayed in this loud, clear, bugle voice. Then she checked herself. "I don't need his money. Monday I'm buying a money order and sending it right back to him. Let him spend it on his Tooth Fairy!" Which really cracked me up. Lou, the Tooth Fairy. I never heard Mom talk this way before. It was always Dad is a good man, and Mom is a good woman, and Lou is a good woman, and all that crap that you knew she didn't mean. So I said as much to her and asked how come she's changed. She got flustered and apologetic. "I shouldn't have talked that way. He *is* a good man, and she *is* a good woman—" She stopped, as if she were groping for words, then looked me in the eye. "But I'm just as good as they are, and don't you forget it!"

We turned onto a side street of bare trees and brownstones, and after walking half a block we were at her apartment building. She lives in the basement. We stepped down from the sidewalk into this pocket-size stone paved area, then Mom unlocked a wrought-iron gate under the wide steps leading to the main door. She made a speech about always locking everything all the time whether I went in or out— gate, hall door, door to her apartment, which is the one in front.

When she opened the door and switched on the light, those three pictures of me when I was a little kid smiled at me. They are smiling at me right now. They are in thin gold frames joined together, standing under silk peach blossoms spreading from a blue-and-white Oriental vase. She told me she stashed the booze money in that vase so she would have to look me in the eye every time she was tempted to dip into it.

As for the rest of the apartment—I remember her with sofas and bedrooms and drapes and like that. But this is just one long, wide room with almost nothing in it. A sofa bed and a big chair with one floor lamp for both. A narrow table under the windows that face the little patio, with two chairs that don't match. She put the table there, even if it is as far as it can get from the kitchen, so she can look out on the little patio and the street and catch the breeze in the summer.

Opposite the door, bookshelves on the wall. My pictures are on the highest shelf. The others hold books and magazines and a little black-and-white TV. The back half of the room is empty. The back wall, the one opposite the windows, has three doors—one to a big closet, another to the kitchen, and the third to the bathroom, all about the same size. Mom loves this place. Says it's safe and clean and warm in winter and she can afford it. Naturally, I wondered where I was going to sleep. She sleeps on the sofa bed. She borrowed a cot for me, which is folded up in the closet. I slept in it last night. I mean I slept in the trench down the middle of it. It has such a deep sag I don't think I'm visible once I go to bed.

The smell of the stew she had made and was warming up, and the real me smiling down from under the peach blossoms, and the big, clean, white-walled room, and her so glad to see me—it was super. We sat side by side at the narrow table, and I told her how delicious the stew was, and she leaned over and kissed me and told me again she couldn't believe I was sitting there with her. Then, radiating at me the way Julie does, she said she jogs every morning, and would I jog with her? I said sure.

The only flies in the ointment—she has a boyfriend—I knew it—and she has started to bug me about my problems. Started last night. After she told me for the eightieth time how handsome I am, and after I told her for the eightieth time she's a knockout, we didn't have anything to say. THE QUESTION hung in the air between us. I concentrated on eating. Finally, in an uncertain voice, Mom said, "Now, what's this all about, Roger, you and that girl—" She looked at me squarely. "Roger, I'm such an outsider in your life. Please let me in. It's taken me a long time to get myself together, but I am together now, and I can help you. Don't be afraid to tell me, honey. I mean who am I to make judgments, with my history? Tell me about it."

I was touched. She is sure different from Dad. We had hit it off so well, and she is so crazy about me, and I thought maybe I would live with her after this school semester, so I started telling her about Carmel.

Just on cue the phone rang. By the way she got all rosy and self-conscious and turned away, I knew immediately. It was him. The boyfriend. Probably another Lou with a sixteen-year-old son who's All-American quarterback going for his Ph.D. in nuclear physics. She turned back to face me.

"Does a chicken have lips? Does a snake have hips?" she asked into the phone, grinning and sparkling. Then she said, "O.K., champ, see you Monday," and hung up.

"What was that jive about the chicken and the snake?" I asked.

"He wanted to know if we'd like to go to Yankee Stadium Monday night, and I was saying yes." She was radiating and giggling. I never saw her that way with Dad. "That's my Joe. He's so funny." I didn't smile. I must have looked pretty sour, because she came back to the table, kissed me, and said, "Sorry about the interruption. Go on, Roger." But I was out of the mood. I told her I was tired—couldn't we wait till tomorrow? She said sure. Said I looked beat. Said we'd just take it easy tonight and watch TV, and I could go to bed whenever I wanted to.

So we sat on the couch holding hands, and I fell asleep just as the vampire was creeping up on this beautiful dame who was sleeping with her bare throat hanging out. Mom made up my cot. I could hardly stay awake long enough to undress.

So this morning Mom was all ready to go. She had been waiting for me for a couple of hours. She says her morning run picks her up and pulls her together and she's ready to face whatever crap the day has in store for her.

I jumped into my clothes and drank some orange juice, and we locked up and joined the swarm of joggers running along our side of the street. Another swarm was jogging in the opposite direction along the other curb. I matched my pace to Mom's, which is slow. She says she never runs so fast that she can't talk, which she does nonstop, but I must say she's in shape. She maintained the same pace jogging and talking for an hour and a half. Reminds me of Julie.

We started off through streets lined with old brownstones like Mom's. Each one is different, but they are all neat and proper with window boxes and carved wood and beveled glass doors. Mom wanted to start a conversation right away. She kept looking at me, but I was busy taking in the old brownstones. There is nothing like them in Del Amo. Old and elegant and up-tight.

Finally she began sort of uncertainly, "You know, Roger, I am very shy with you. Last time I was with you you were still a kid—my kid—" Her voice took on that old, apologetic, whiny tone. "Oh, Roger, you don't know how I hated not being a real mother to you." Her voice broke the way it used to, and I said, the way I used to, "That's O.K., Mom."

But she shook her head and went on. "But now look at

you! You're tall and handsome and a *young man*—and I don't know how to talk to you, and you have problems." She looked at me, begging. "Roger dearest—tell me about your girl—"

"She *isn't* my girl, Mom!" I really didn't want to talk about Carmel or anything else to do with Del Amo, but while we doubled back and forth among the brownstones, and ran for a while on a wide street with Arab stores, I told her how I used to bump into Julie in the field when she was walking her dog and I was walking Pippa, and how her sister is in my English class and she got pregnant by this dude who also used to be in my English class—

"Friend of yours?"

"That jerk? No way!" She looked confused and started to ask a question, but before she could, I went on about how Gene moved away and Carmel's girl friend's car was totaled by the drunk before she was to drive Carmel to the hospital, and she was in the hospital herself, and how Carmel was going to kill herself so I said I'd drive her, and how I had a hell of a time getting the van from that fink Vanessa, and Dad found out, and how we were having a knock-down drag-out the night she called, but that everything turned out all right.

"What do you mean, turned out all right? You're here now instead of July because everything turned out all right?"

"Well, I mean Carmel had the abortion on time," I said.

I just didn't want to talk about it. I wanted to look at Brooklyn, and I wasn't as sure as I was last night that she would understand. Her interest lies with Joe.

But she plowed ahead. "Do you still see her?"

"Sure. She's in my English class."

"You see her only in English? You took her for an abortion, and you only see her in English?"

I shrugged.

"I don't get a clear picture," she said. "I just don't get a clear picture at all."

By this time we were approaching the Promenade, a wide strolling area hanging over the East River. When we reached it, I stopped running and leaned against the wrought-iron fence and gazed at the island of Manhattan floating down the river toward the open sea. She carried a cargo of towers and shafts, erect rectangles, spires, low, squat buildings all gilded by the morning sun. She looked like a dream. Upriver, the superstructure of the Brooklyn Bridge swooped and dipped between its towers. Just below me a freighter from Rio rested quietly on the water. Because it was Sunday, the piers and docks on both sides of the river were deserted and still. Semi-trailer containers of cargo stacked like huge boxes; trucks, winches, cranes, and coiled cables the size of my wrist silently waited for Monday.

My gaze wandered toward the New Jersey shore. There she was off the tip of Manhattan—the Old Lady on her pedestal holding up her torch! Even at this distance I could see that she didn't give a damn about anything except holding up that torch for everyone who passed by. Nothing, but nothing could upstage her, not even the two incredible shafts of the World Trade Center.

Finally I let go of the iron spikes, and Mom and I started jogging again. She had not stopped talking. While we descended to the river's edge, she told me her brilliant idea about the hundred bucks Dad gave me to spend. Said she's never again going to take a plugged penny from him, but that's her problem, not mine.

"He gave the money to you, too. I know a little shop in the Village where they sell ceramic jewelry that looks like a lot more than what you pay for it. You can bring presents, so you won't look selfish, and then keep the rest for dates, or whatever you want. I want you to tell him that we didn't spend a cent of his money on me. You hear?" I said O.K. "We can get your father one of those corny tie tacks he loves, and some ducky-yucky dangly earrings for the Tooth Fairy—" She made a retching sound. It's times like this when I like her best. "And what for Vanessa?" she asked.

We were standing under the Brooklyn Bridge, and I was listening to it vibrate from traffic like a loud, off-key violin. "Poisoned toilet paper," I said absentmindedly.

This stopped Mom—both talking and jogging. She cracked up. She laughed so hard she bent over double, while I stood grinning, waiting for her, pleased with myself for being so comical.

We circled back to Montague Street, which reminds me a little of San Francisco. We were famished. We ate at a place with ferns and old copper and pewter, but the food was good, and there was lots of it.

Dad just phoned. I have the abandoned cat feeling again. What if I were to stay here for good? I can probably handle Mom more easily than I can Dad. At least enough to live with for a few months or a year or so till I am eighteen and can be on my own. I'd have to have Pippa, even though Dad says she doesn't act as if she missed me. She just doesn't show her feelings. He and Lou are going away until Thursday. He will call then.

Tomorrow I will be by myself in Manhattan. While we were eating, Mom told me what's happening. Since this is the final week before the tax deadline, there is no way she can get time off. She works for this big accounting firm. She'll be lucky to get a half holiday Good Friday. So I'm going to work with her tomorrow and explore midtown Manhattan and meet her for lunch, and of course we are going to the ball game tomorrow night. I wish it were just the two of us. Joe is going to be a pain in the ass. I just know.

It will be neat to explore by myself. Mom and I are getting along a lot better than I thought we would, but she talks too much, and she's always in there, digging, trying to get at the bottom of My Problem. Like when we were walking home from brunch, she said to me, "I gather you're not crazy about Vanessa."

"She's a bitch," I said.

"Why?" I didn't want to go into all that and wreck my day, so I just shrugged. "What does your father think about her?"

"She has him eating out of her hand. He thinks she's perfect," I said. Mom waited for me to go on, but I didn't. She let the subject drop, though I know she has it filed away for future reference. She said, sliding her eyes over to me slyly, "Where do you go when you date, honey?"

"Mom, I don't date."

She didn't believe me. "Come on! A handsome boy like you!"

"It's the haircut," I told her. "Usually I look like a wimpy sheepdog."

"Roger," she begged, "how can I convince you to trust me? I hate being three thousand miles out of your life."

So why did she walk out on me?

I told her, "I trust you, Mom. I told you everything." Does she seriously think she can solve My Problem in a week? Man, I've spent sixteen years perfecting it.

"Don't you see, I'm trying to understand? Flunking out of school, and this abortion thing...and you were such a good responsible little kid...in the mentally gifted program at Schofield Elementary—"

"Schofield was a long time ago," I told her. "Besides, I'm only borderline in English, and I can make it up, and Dad has hired a tutor for me in chemistry."

But she just looked at me with sad eyes, like a hound dog that's been beaten. "What's wrong, Roger?" she asked.

What a question! How can I tell her about the holocausts of rage at her and Dad and Lou and Vanessa burning inside of me? How can I tell her about the boulders of Disaster Data about to fall on me, the mountains of Disaster Data about to fall on the whole world? And through all this, bits of English and chemistry and social studies float down like snowflakes, melting before they even reach me.

Anyway, I'm going to have a good week. Later on I'll go farther after I know my way around a little. She's got a good map, and she'll tell me how to get where I want to go and where to stay away from.

Actually, I only got to the part about the Statue of Liberty when Mom came back with the deli. The rest I have been writing in the little closet, sitting on the floor. There is an overhead light, and I closed the door. I can't sleep. Nights have always been hard for me. I guess I'll get back into the trench, though. My butt is cold and probably flat from sitting on the floor so long.

Tuesday, April 10

Grounded.

It's raining, and I have a rotten cold. She's glad. Of course, she wouldn't say so, but I could see the relief in her eyes when she kissed me good-bye. She will know where I am all day. As if I were a five-year-old. So I was a couple hours late. Big deal. When I knew I couldn't make it for lunch, I did call her, didn't I? Then, coming back, I didn't want to take the time to find a phone and get later still. I don't see why she gets so hysterical. You'd think I had committed a string of felonies. All I did was walk when I should have caught a cab or the subway. I tried to get a cab, but the suckers wouldn't stop for me, and I was afraid I'd end up in New Jersey or the West Bronx or somewhere if I took the wrong subway. So I walked back from Chinatown, and it took longer than I figured.

I really started out to walk down Fifth Avenue to 32nd Street and then over to Madison Square Garden and then back to her office for lunch. That's what the plans were. Then this afternoon I was supposed to amble over to the UN or check out Central Park and be at her office by five to go to the ball game with her and Joe. Only I didn't get back to her office till about seven.

What happened was I never even knew when I got to 32nd Street. In the first place, when I was all by myself, I was cold-cocked by the noise—a building falling down behind a wooden barricade, a giant generator roaring, a million buses, trucks, taxis, and all over the place these black limos honking, braking, accelerating; traffic cops tweetling, sirens screaming, jackhammers drilling right into my skull. And the sidewalks were jammed. Wherever I stood to get my bearings, I was in somebody's way. Two streams going in opposite directions with eddies and interminglings, the whole current damming up at street corners waiting for traffic signals. Traffic jams—complete stoppage in four directions—then movement and the jam disappears. Incredible. And everybody is on an urgent mission—on foot or in vehicles. No nonsense. *Get outta my way!* I was sucked into the wakes of these jokers who knew where they were going, and I followed automatically.

Then there were the buildings! Fantastic masses of concrete and glass, great surges of upward energy, manipulating the light of day, the air currents, the noise splashing and pounding and shattering against them. I am a dot, an ant, a moving grease spot, a drop in a stream of humanity swirling around their bases.

So I walked and walked, losing all track of time and distance, always in a crowd, always battered by noise. From Brooklyn Heights Manhattan looks like a solid wall of tall, shining buildings, but when you get into the middle of it, you see that most of them are lower, and there are parks, which sort of open things up and let the light in. And you see that most of the buildings are old. At street level many of them are painted and remodeled, but above the second story they are dirty and seem to be gradually crumbling. New York is basically *old*. Del Amo is basically *new*. Manhattan is up and packed together. In Del Amo people take their time when they walk. They hurry only when they drive. The sidewalks are empty, but the streets are jammed with cars. Here there are crowds of people and crowds of cars, and everyone is in a hurry. In Del Amo smog blurs colors and lines. Here, even though the air stinks of exhaust, the atmosphere is clear.

The time, running around in an electric sign on top of a building, shocked me out of my daze. Twelve-ten, and I was supposed to have been at Mom's office at 11:45. I looked for a phone booth, but I had to go a few blocks before I found one. On a dingy street hung with banners with Oriental writing I found a phone booth in the shape of a Chinese pagoda. While I waited for Mom to come on the line, I watched Oriental dudes rushing and dodging each other or blocking the sidewalk while they bought fish out of buckets, fruit out of crates, clothing from card tables—or almost anything out of parked vans.

"Where are you!!"

Mom's screech made me wince. I held the phone away from my ear and told her I was on Canal Street.

"Canal Street! You're in Chinatown! How did you get to Chinatown?"

"I just started walking. I don't want you to worry about me, because I won't be able to make it for lunch."

"Thanks a lot! You were supposed to be here at quarter to twelve. You promised to stay close! Why did you go to Chinatown?"

"I told you. I just started walking. I'm O.K., Mom."

"But I'm not! I'm wild! Your first time alone in the city! Now, listen to me! You catch a cab and get back here—" Which apparently reminded her of something. *"Roger Judd, do you still have your wallet?"* she screams. I tell her I still have my wallet, while she is yelling about how worried she has been, and telling me how to get back, how I wrecked her lunch hour, etc., etc. Finally I said I'd see her at four-thirty, and hung up. I really meant to be there, too.

I bought myself a hamburger and a Pepsi and ate while I walked. I lost half my Pepsi when a little old lady in black pj's joggled my elbow in her rush to the shrimp bucket, so I slid over to the storefronts to get out of the way. I looked into the funky Chinese store windows at tea and herbs and pale, knobby vegetables, silks, fans, paper lanterns, jade, naked ducks and chickens hanging upside down. I passed a hardware store, and among dusty hand tools and kitchen stuff in a dusty corner of the window, an army of horny toads glared at me. Warty brown and cream and green ceramic toads. I flashed on that day in the field with the dogs running through the pond and the horny toads hugging and jumping and Julie and me catching that pair. I almost burst out laughing, and I thought what a crack-up it would be to buy a couple and glue one on top of the other and keep them on my desk.

So I went into this crowded, noisy hardware store and tried to get up nerve to ask someone to wait on me. After a while I asked this old character in a sweater for two toads and got yelled at. He barked at me, but he got two toads out of the window, wrapped them in Chinese newspaper, put them in a bag, and took my money without interrupting a loud conversation or argument he was having with another old guy in a raincoat.

When I came out of the hardware store, I tried to flag down a cab, but no luck. It was only two o'clock, so I took my map and pinpointed where I was and decided to walk back. I should have gone back exactly the way I came—up

Broadway to Fifth Avenue and right on up—but I got side-tracked and found myself in Little Italy, so I checked out the stores where they sell pastries or meat or vegetables or pictures of Jesus bleeding.

I was getting hungry, since I only had one hamburger and half a Pepsi, so I ducked in and got a slice of pizza, and coffee, and it was good, so I had another piece and then some kind of pastry made with whipped cream and chocolate. So when I started out again, I was kind of logy, and it took a while for me to hit my stride, and I was farther east than I thought—so all in all it took me a lot longer to get back to 56th Street and Fifth Avenue than it had to get down to Canal Street.

So it was quarter to seven when I opened the door to the office where Mom works. And she was crying, and this short-ish, baldish guy with a small potbelly had one arm around her, and he was stroking her head. When he saw me he got red and jumped away from her.

"Here he is," he said cheerfully. "I told you he'd show up without a scratch." He came over to me, holding out his hand. Looking over my left shoulder, he said, "Joe Slay." We shook hands. "You sure had your mom worried," he said to the filing cabinet behind me.

Meanwhile, Mom had rushed over. "Honest to God, I don't know whether to kill you or kiss you!" she said in this weepy, laughy voice. "Where were you?" I told her I walked back, and it took me a long time. "*Why? Why* did you *walk?*" I shrugged. Her expression began to sour.

"I tried to flag down a cab, but the creeps wouldn't stop for me," I told her.

"You sure didn't try very hard," she said. "Why didn't

you phone me when you knew you were going to be so late?"

"I didn't want to waste time looking for a phone. I just wanted to get here."

She got sarcastic. "Where in the world do you think you are? Out in the backwoods? In the middle of the desert? All you had to do was go into any drugstore or restaurant—"

I was feeling guilty and mad at myself for being such a dud, so I snarled, "God, you'd think I committed some kind of crime! All I did was walk—"

Joe put his arm around Mom. "Listen, Carole, you gotta face facts. This kid's a walker. Some kids are dopers, some kids are drinkers, you got a walker. You're just going to have to learn to live with it. Let's eat."

Then it turned out that I have wrecked their plans for eating at a fantastic Italian restaurant where they made reservations and everything. We had just time to get to the ball park and eat hot dogs. Mom was furious. All that love and goodwill we had going yesterday—fffft!—gone like a balloon someone stuck a pin into. We rushed down to the subway and caught a train. Joe has a car, but like a lot of people here, he uses it only when he has to, on account of the traffic and the parking. I was thinking if we had buses and subways in Del Amo like they do here, Carmel would have had no problem getting to the hospital.

By that time I was really bushed. I dozed off in the train in spite of the racket and in spite of the fact that I was standing up. I didn't really wake up till we surfaced right by the stadium.

Our seats were in the very upper deck past the foul poles in right field. We could see everything. Yankee Stadium is a nice ball park. They do instant replays on the scoreboard.

Joe considers the place holy ground. "You're sitting in the midst of history, Roger," he tells the air over my left shoulder. Yankees vs. Angels. Yankees 3–0. They take Trevor out in the seventh. He pitched a good game, but Joe called him your basic schlemiel. He is so prejudiced he makes me sick.

It was a good game and all, but I didn't want to be there. I was tired and cold, and my throat was getting sore. That damned wind cut like a knife. I gave Mom a splitting headache, and she sat with a sour face hardly talking to me. On the other side of her that paunchy squirt kept throwing out a never-ending stream of corny one-liners to cheer her up, but he finally gave up—he held her hand and watched the game in silence. I sat and froze. I didn't belong. I cramped their style, screwed up their evening.

I was supposed to go into Manhattan again this morning, but it's pouring, and my throat is on fire. I really screwed up what Mom and I had going between us. This morning she was polite but distant. She looked bad. I can see her point. I was more than two hours late, and I guess some parts of Manhattan are a real jungle, and she was worried. I really should have phoned. I'll apologize tonight.

But I don't really belong here, either. Mom's got things worked out with Joe and she needs me like she needs a hole in the head. Brooklyn Heights with Joe or 200th Street in Del Amo with Lou and Vanessa? It makes no difference. I'm always in other people's houses.

Dear Roger:
I wanted to say more than I could on that silly card, but now I don't know how to say it. You changed my

life. Your courage and humanity showed me what a shallow, superficial person I am. You stuck your neck out when I asked you to. You had nothing to gain. You weren't in love with me or Carmel or anything like that. Not even a friend at first. You helped because we needed you. You are a fine human being.

I wrote this poem. You inspired it. It is a declaration of my new self. I am going to conquer my cowardice. I hope you like it.

> You twin bullies—Life and Death
> Come! I call your bluff.
> I'm ready for you.
>
> For too long you bullies
> Have held your weapons
> Over my head
>
> And I cowered and whimpered
> Fearing the club
> And the scythe.
>
> Now the hell with both of you!
> Life, your hollow
> Promises and threats
>
> Can lead but to Death
> And, Death, you are
> An empty nothing!

Wednesday, April 11

I was looking through my tote for my ticket so I could call and confirm my reservation home, and I dropped *The Treason Trust*, and it fell open where the letter was shoved way back in the book. I think she likes me.

My throat is a lot better, but it's still pouring and cold. Mom melted last night when I told her I was sorry, but says this is no weather for a thin-blooded Californian with a cold to be out in.

Julie's every bit as good-looking as Carmel. The only thing Carmel has going for her is the nose.

"You changed my life. Your courage and humanity"—hey, that's me she's talking about. "You are a fine human being." Here I've been living with you for sixteen years, creep, and never knew. We have had a lot of laughs, Julie and I. And that time she gave me the poppy . . .

Dear Julie:

I read your letter and the poem. I didn't know you were a poet. Ever since I met you I don't know what to expect. At first I thought you were weird, but the longer I know you—I just never know what to think. You say I changed your life. Man, what about what you did to mine. All those wild things that happened to me since I first saw you—almost getting shot, getting mixed up with Carmel's abortion, and now, a poem. I can't wait to get back to Del Amo.

My Darling, My Dearest, My Angel, I am a thousand-piece band playing "Looking for My Love." I am Superdude—no, Superdud—juggling the sun and the moon for you. I have to see you. I will kiss you all over—the little hollow at the base of your throat, your adorable squashed nose, your eyes, your ears, your mouth

Hey, wait a minute. Slow down. Take it easy.

Dear Julie:

I read your letter and the poem. I didn't know you were a poet, but ever since I met you I don't know what to expect. I look forward to seeing you when I come home Sunday.

Yours sincerely,
Roger Judd

My Dearest Julie. My Sweet.

I am back from mailing my letter to you, and I am writing you again because I can't stop thinking about you. I have put on dry clothes and stashed my wet shoes and jeans in the oven. If my Mom knew what I did, she would be wild. I have this rotten cold, and it is pouring. I had to get the letter off to you. I had to. I figured I would only need to go to the corner, but naturally the drugstore was out of stamps, so I had to go to the post office, about three blocks away in the pouring rain. It is an immense old gray stone government building with revolving doors. Do you know about revolving doors? The trick is to jump into the little space behind one that is running away from you before the next one cracks you from the rear. I stand there in the downpour watching old folks, cripples, ablebodied types step in and disappear. Finally I get on my mark, get set, jump in behind and in the same section with an enormous black guy with an enormous Afro all sparkly with raindrops, only he doesn't know I'm there. I'm afraid of being trapped and having to go around in circles forever, so in my panic I tread on his heels and fall against him when we get out. His hands shoot up over his head as if I had a gun to his back, and he does not look behind. I say, "Pardon me," and he drops his hands, turns around, grins, says, "No problem," and hightails it away! Isn't that wild?

I bought my stamp and would have kissed your letter before I dropped it in the chute, but there were too many people. I wished you were with me so we could run through the rain together. Would you let me hold your hand? Maybe kiss you while we wait for the light to change? We would laugh at the beat-up umbrellas. You never see a decent umbrella here. They are beaten up by the wind, which blows them inside out. Different from Del Amo, where people don't walk farther than across the parking lot if they can help it, rain or shine, and the umbrellas are always new.

I've made myself some sandwiches, and I'm eating at Mom's table under the windows, which are a little below street level. All I can see are feet and legs. There is a constant procession. These crazy New Yorkers don't know enough to come in out of the rain. Remember, we got soaked the day we buried the gopher? Hey, guess what I got for you in Chinatown Monday. Two ceramic horny toads. Horny toads—we are the only people in the world who know what that means. I can't wait to give them to you, my shrimpy sexpot.

Just caught the noon news. My darling, is the news a downer for you, too? I call it Disaster Data. Today's DD item is that we are going to starve by the year 2000 because population growth will outstrip food production.

Thursday, April 12

I never thought she was capable of such a rotten, dirty, mean trick. She has left her keys with me in case of fire. Thanks a lot, Mom. What I need is my pants. She took both pairs. Said it was either shoes or pants and after yesterday, she figured pants were a better bet. Said I'll get them back when I tell her where I went yesterday and what I was doing Monday.

And it's all because I'm such a jerk. Creep! Nerd! Dud!

I forgot to take my jeans and shoes out of the oven. When she opened the oven door to put in the casserole—that's when it hit the fan.

What are these clothes doing in here? How did you get your clothes wet? Where did you go? In this rain? With your cold?

Where did I go? To the post office. Why? All I could come up with on the spur of the moment was my old friend—the guy on crutches with V.D. So I gave her this b.s. about a dude who let me use his car, and we forgot to set a place to leave the key when I parked it in front of his house, and I tried to call before I left but couldn't reach him, then I forgot about it till yesterday, and he has to use the car tomorrow to get to a doctor's appointment, and he'll never think to look where I put it on the chassis behind the left front wheel, so I had to send him a special delivery letter. Of course she didn't buy.

"Roger, this is the second time this week, and you said it

would never happen again. What's going on? Where did you go? I won't get mad. I didn't know where you were Monday, but now I see you are safe. I just want to know where you went. What's so urgent to get you out in this rain when you're burning up with fever?"

"I told you the truth, honest, Mom," I lied.

"Roger, level with me. Are you hooked on anything?" For a second the words didn't register. "Are you an alcoholic?"

"No!" I yelled.

"You've had it rough—with me leaving—Dad—Lou—Vanessa—and you're a lot like me, and sometimes a drink or a joint or a pill makes life bearable—"

"Mom, I'm not hooked on anything!" I also wanted to yell, "I am *not* like you. I want to be like Dad," but of course I didn't.

She began to cry. "Oh, Roger, if you knew how I hate myself for not being a real mother to you! Let me help you, Roger."

It would have made things so much easier for her if I had been hooked, but I wasn't. All I could do was pat her on the shoulder and say, "You're my real mother, Mom. Put the casserole in the oven so we can eat."

She dried her eyes and made dinner. As soon as we sat down, she said, "Where did you go today, honey?"

So we dragged through the whole thing again during dinner and after dinner and all night until we went to bed. And right in the middle, Dad phoned, the way Mom did the night he and I had the big fight. He and Lou were just back from Big Bear and he wanted to check in. Mom jumped on him for sending me here in April without a warm jacket, told him I practically have pneumonia. He apparently asked her why hadn't she gotten off her duff and bought me one, and they had a good fight. He was still mad when I talked to him. Ordered me to go to a doctor tomorrow. Ordered me to confirm my reservation for Sunday. I told him I already had. Fine. See you one-fifteen Sunday. Good-bye. Slam!

What with all the fighting and tension, I expected Mom to disappear into the bathroom or the closet, or go to the fridge for something cold, the way she used to, but she didn't even take a drink of water. Only lots of coffee, and I know it was coffee, because I had it, too.

Dearest Love—

This is another letter you will never get. I need someone to listen to me today and to laugh at my jokes, though I don't feel very comical today. I am in my native Miseryland. I need you to take my hand and lead me out.

I forgot and left my wet clothes in the oven. I was in the middle of the letter I wrote you when I got back from the post office. The timer went off, and I just shut off the gas and came back to you, meaning to take my clothes out later, but I forgot. So my mom found them and wanted to know why I went out in the rain with a cold. I can't tell her about us, can I? She thinks I'm hooked and needed a fix or a drink or something. She used to have a drinking problem, and she's afraid like mother like son. So she takes my pants to work with her every day to keep me from getting into trouble. Today and tomorrow and Saturday. I hope I can last that long.

I mean it is pretty humiliating to be in New York grounded with no pants. My only ray of hope and sunshine is that in three and a half days I will see you.

Or will I? Julie, will you really love me when I get back to Del Amo? And if you do, will it be forever? Look at my mom and dad and Carmel and Gene, and we could think of fifty others, I bet.

I guess I am looking for something that will be forever in a world that is going down the drain. Did you know they are cutting a thousand trees a day in the Amazon forest? And the whales are almost gone and so are the grizzlies and the condors—and we're even running out of land to grow food on.

I made up a poem for you last night when I couldn't sleep. It isn't as good as yours.

> Fly to the east, fly to the west.
> Fly away, baby, to the place you like best.
> Got news for you, baby, whatever your route.
> Disaster's gonna get you without a doubt.

Friday the thirteenth

Big deal. How can it be worse than Thursday the twelfth? Or Wednesday the eleventh? I couldn't bear it if I didn't know that day after tomorrow I'll be on the plane back to Del Amo. She took them again this morning. She's so damned sneaky and quick. One second she's here, the next second she's out the door. She even hides them somewhere when we go to bed. Some trust in her son. I meant to get up in the middle of the night and find them and sleep on top of them, but I slept through. A guy shouldn't have to fight his mother for his own pants. It's humiliating. It's insane. I can't believe how she has changed. Used to sit around and cry and drink herself blind. Now she's sober and mean. I have looked all over in every nook and corner for her bottle, but either she really is sober or she carries it with her like my pants.

Yesterday she came home dripping forgiveness and phony cheer. Said, look, we only have another three nights together. Let's be friends. I didn't say anything, let my arms hang when she hugged and kissed me. "Let's go to the show tonight, honey. *Moonster* is playing a few blocks away. We can walk. O.K.?"

All I said was, "Give me my pants."

Her face fell, but what did she expect? She handed me my jeans, saying I would feel better after I ate. I slammed the bathroom door and gave it a good kick in answer. All through dinner she bubbled happy talk. I didn't say a word.

After dinner we walked the few blocks to the movie. Actually, I had seen it already in Del Amo, but I wasn't going to enter into even that much conversation with her, and anyway, seeing it again was better than sitting around the apartment with her. But I didn't laugh. Didn't even move. Went into my complete totem pole act. At first she was enjoying the picture, but after a while she stopped laughing. Kept looking at me. I ruined the show for her. Serves her right.

But that woman never gives up. On the way home, she tucked her arm through mine and said, "Roger, stop acting like a child. We've got to talk. You're here because you have problems."

I said, "Leave me alone. Everything's all taken care of."

"Don't give me that crap!" she snapped, the sweetness finally cracking. "Why did your father practically throw you out? Why are you here now instead of later when I wanted you to come, if you have no problems?"

"We got everything settled before I came. When you talked to him we were in the middle of a big fight. We worked it out after—"

"That's not the way I heard it. The way I heard it, your father is at his wits' end because you got some girl pregnant and you're flunking out of school—"

"I didn't get anyone pregnant!" I yell at her. "And he's going to hire a tutor for me, and I'm not going to ditch school any more, and everything's settled! I've told you a million times!"

"So there's no problem?"

"No."

"Come on! Do you think I was born yesterday? You're never at school, you take some girl for an abortion, you won't account for hours of your time here in New York—*Roger, you have problems!*"

I ran away from her. I ran all the way home. It felt good after having been in jail for three days.

When she got to the gate under the stairs, she said, "You might as well get it through your head that you're going to talk to me before you leave. No pants tomorrow."

So here I am, contemplating my knees. I wonder if I can stand even two more days of this.

Dearest Julie—

Got your number from Information and had my finger on the dial but chickened out. Suppose your mom answered? Suppose *you* answered? I mean, what would I say? I don't even know for sure that you love me. Maybe the letter and the poem are your weird way of saying thanks for everything, good-bye, and good luck. I decided I couldn't risk it. I have to go on thinking that you love me—at least until I get back to Del Amo and see you face to face. What will I see on that gorgeous, flat-nosed, adorable little face? Oh, Julie, I hope you like me.

It's raining again. If you were here with me, I would love you. I think I had trouble with that kiss because it was so unexpected, the day you gave me the poppy. I assure you there will be no problem with kisses. . . . If you were here, we would look out the window together and you would tell me that the drops running down the panes were rain crystals. Without you, they look like tears. I just saw a dachshund wearing a rain cape and moccasins, attached to a pair of plump jeans with a pooper scooper. Tell Butchie.

I just reread your poem. I see you lighting up a scary

black void just by being there, smiling, radiating. I see hovering over you these two big threatening shapes like those nerds with the rifles only bigger and scarier because they are Life and Death. Through the darkness comes your high squeak—"To hell with both of you!" I jump behind *you*, because you are braver than I am now.

I love you.

Roger

Saturday, April 14

Friday the thirteenth *was* worse than Thursday the twelfth. Much worse. The evening started out like Thursday with her trying to make up. Brought home filet mignon. Says it's my next to last night here, and this has been a rotten trip, and we might as well have a couple good meals, at least. She looks terrible. Says she will have to work tomorrow (today, Saturday) she hopes only half a day, but they have had equipment failure and every other kind of trouble, and if they don't get those tax returns finished, she will have to work Sunday, too. Joe will take me to the airport. She cusses out Dad for sending me at such a bad time. Says she's sorry that what little time we had together was so unpleasant.

When I answered by holding out my hand for my pants, her face crumpled into crying, and I felt like a real heel. I took a long shower and spent a lot of time in the bathroom, because I didn't want to face her.

When we sat down to eat, Mom said, "I didn't see us like this, Roger. I figured you'd come in summer, and we'd have a lot of fun—" Her voice got wobbly. "You don't know how often I think about you. I can see you have no idea how much you mean to me. You don't know how it feels to be on the outside looking in—" Deep silence from me. She blew up. "I deserve better than this! Being treated like some snoopy aunt or cousin trying to butt in! *I'm your mother!*"

I've had all I can take. I'm sick of her. All of a sudden she's my mother.

"Oh, yeah?" I yelled back. "Where have you been for the last eight years? One week every summer? That should make you my mother?" Eight years of rage flamed behind the resentment I feel about my pants. "And giving me all that crap about how Dad is a good man and you're a good woman, and you both love me, and how lucky I am to have a good home with Lou and Vanessa—bull! You ran out on me!"

"Stop yelling at me! You ought to get down on your knees and thank me. Do you remember what it was like to live with a drunk? How you'd come home from school, stick your head in the door, and say, 'Mom, you O.K.?' and if I wasn't blubbering in the recliner with a bottle, you'd tell Mike from next door he could come in? And how you never brought anyone else from school to your house? Do you remember the fights your father and I had—the miserable days and nights?"

I remember the fights—how I would hide in the closet. I remember how ashamed I was for anyone to see her, how I helped her do things she was too drunk to do, the smell of her, the feel of her teary cheek when she kissed me. But I also remembered that *she had been there*, that my father came home to us at night, that I slept in my own bedroom, played on my own block, went to my own school.

I said to her, "I remember there was no one home any more, and I wore dirty clothes to school, and we ate junk. But *he* was there when I cried for you!"

"My God, how you hate me!" She clenched her fists across her chest, dropped into her chair like a rock. I do hate her. I also hate the little phony smiling down at us from under the fake peach blossoms. I hate most of all the creep, the dud, the nothing he has grown up to be.

Mom and I sat looking at the filets as if we were reading bad news written all over them. After a while she went to the closet and got her coat and bag.

"Where are you going?" I asked. All of a sudden I was filled with panic.

"Out," she said, not looking at me.

I knew where she was headed, and it was my fault. I had gone too far.

"Mom, I'm sorry—"

She faced me, stony, wrinkled, stooped. "Be honest," she said. "We can never be close, because you'll never forgive me for leaving." Her voice was husky but steady. She turned to the door, muttering, "I was kidding myself."

"Wait for me!" I hurried to the closet for my jacket.

"Let me live my life, and I'll let you live yours," she said. I took her arm. We went through the gate and onto the sidewalk. As I expected, we were heading straight for the liquor store. I took a deep breath.

"Mom, suppose I told you I did get Carmel pregnant and that I am hooked on booze?"

She stopped in front of the liquor store and faced me.

"After all you've put me through you're telling me that now?" she said bitterly.

"No, I didn't say that." I gently pulled her past the liquor store. "I said *suppose*."

"What does that mean? What do I care about suppose?"

"But, Mom, why do you want to believe that I got Carmel pregnant, that I'm an alcoholic? Why won't you believe the truth?"

"What truth? The truth is whatever you want to believe—like I just picked up and walked out on you. Like I deserted you—"

"You don't know how it hurt. I was just a little kid—"

She says, "There is this particular kind of bull kids believe that only kids can be hurt."

"But I thought it was my fault. I didn't know what was going on. I was just a little *kid*—"

She yanked her arm away and covered her face with her hands and began to sob. "I know it! And so vulnerable—and I'm so sorry—but, Roger, I didn't know what else to do! I was fighting for my life!"

"I know, Mom," I said, and gave her a quick hug. She wiped her eyes, blew her nose, and we turned back toward the apartment. The danger was over.

"O.K.," she said, putting her arm through mine and hugging it, "I didn't desert you, and you didn't get What's-her-face pregnant, and you are not hooked. Where were you Monday and Wednesday?"

I didn't have the strength. I just told her straight out about finding Julie's letter and poem in the book. For once she just listened. Maybe she ran out of strength, too.

When I finished, she said, "Sixteen...I remember sixteen. I hid the letters from my first love under the floor in my closet. No one knows to this day that I pried up a floor board. . . . And I *lived* with my parents and loved them dearly. Considering our relationship and your opinion of me. . . ." Her voice trailed off.

I felt this incredible sense of relief, as if I had learned I am not crazy. I started talking, and I couldn't stop. All the way back to the apartment and while we finished our cold steak and drank hot coffee, I told her the whole story about Carmel and the abortion, which led to Vanessa and how things are between Dad and me.

"And I thought it was peaches-and-cream paradise over there. I was afraid you'd like Lou better than me—"

"Fat chance," I scoffed.

Mom smiled triumphantly. "—and wouldn't you know that the Tooth Fairy would produce a rotten fang!" Then Mom got serious again. "Listen, Roger, I can understand why your father is worried about you—he does love you, Roger. He always has, from the second he set eyes on you. He may not show it, but he is crazy about you."

"If he's so crazy about me, what about Lou? What about Vanessa? What about him acting as if he's ashamed of me?"

Mom shrugged and looked away. Her face sagged. "Roger, there's a lot about your father I don't understand. If I did, we'd probably still be married. What he sees in that fat Tooth Fairy is one of life's deep mysteries to me. But one thing I *am* sure of. He'll always stand by you."

She pushed back her chair to go to the kitchen—for eclairs. She and I have always had this thing for eclairs ever since I was a kid.

"Why did you say to me, 'What if I got Carmel pregnant?' and so on?" she called from the kitchen."

"Well, I had to get you away from the liquor store," I said, blushing.

She came back with a plate in each hand containing a whipped cream eclair. "I wasn't going to the liquor store. I was going to phone my sponsor, and I couldn't talk to her with you around because I was going to talk about you." She sat down. "I call her every time I need a drink or feel that things are too much for me. This is the first time in four months I've had to call her. Haven't you noticed that I've changed?" Suddenly she got mad. "What in the rosy red hell does it take to prove that a person has changed? I told you I've been dry for twenty-one months! Don't you believe me?"

"I'm sorry, Mom," I mumbled. "I didn't think about it much. You did take my pants," I said accusingly.

"Absolutely. And I've noticed that no man thinks straight with his pants off," Mom said, and we cracked up.

"What got you off the booze?" I asked when we calmed down.

Mom poured another cup of coffee for each of us. We must have had six cups apiece last night. I'm still wired. Anyway, she had this sour smile on her face when she answered, "Your father. When he told me a year ago last July at the airport just before I left that he was going to marry Lou in October. There would be no place for me to come with the rent paid and a full refrigerator. If I wanted to come again, I'd have to make my own arrangements. I never thought he would marry anyone else. I was even more shocked and humiliated than when he divorced me."

"I didn't know he divorced you—I always thought you divorced him," I said.

"Remember, I came back to you guys four months after I left, and we were all together for about a month and a half, and all the bad things started happening again, including the drinking? Actually, I had never stopped. Anyway, that was when he divorced me. That should have told me something, that as far as he was concerned, I was out of his life, but for six years longer I waited for him to ask me back again. Every summer when I came, I hoped and expected to be asked to stay. I told myself that *this time* I'd really stop drinking for good, once we got back together.

"He put an end to all that nonsense that Sunday in July, year before last. When I left that day, I didn't care whether I went on living or not. Didn't know when I was going to see you again. You would have a mother and a home and I wouldn't be needed. Had no money. Unable to hold a job. Living with my parents like an overage teenage drunk. No use to anyone. I really couldn't see any good reason to go on." Mom leaned toward me. "You don't know how it feels—"

"Yes, I do, Mom. I almost hanged myself a couple weeks ago." She almost spilled her coffee as she slammed down her cup. All her wrinkles rushed back into her face. She grabbed my hands. "Oh, dear God, *no!*" she said. Then she let me go and said, "Tell me about it."

So I did. When I finished, she said, "You can't stay there. I'll have to find a larger place—"

I began to squirm and sweat. I am (ongoing condition) really sold on Mom now, but how do I know that things with Joe will be any better than what I have with Lou? I might bitch about Dad, but I know how it will be with him. And I'll be eighteen soon. Besides, there is Julie—or I hope there is Julie—

"I have to finish school," I mumbled.

"But how do I know you won't try again?"

"Don't worry, Mom. That's over. I'm not going to go that

route again. Things are getting too interesting—"

"But what if you and Julie don't work out?"

I looked away, because I don't know what I'd do.

"Roger, what will you do if you feel that low again?"

I shrugged.

"Roger, promise me that you'll call me—at work, at home, any time of the day or night. Promise?"

I nod.

"I'll send you a ticket to come here, right away! And if you can't reach me for some reason, promise you'll talk to someone in Del Amo—Try your father, but if you don't trust him, a help line, a Free Clinic—do your father and Lou go to church?"

"Sometimes."

"But keep calling me, because I want to help you. Do you hear me?"

I nodded and promised I'd phone her, and I probably will, too, if I need to. She's the last person in the world I thought I could trust. Weird.

Sunday, April 15

Here I am again, looking out the window at the pod hanging from the wing. That's all I can see. We are flying through soup. I got cheated out of the Manhattan skyline both times. We came in through clouds and we left through clouds.

Yesterday I slept almost all morning. We didn't get to bed till three-thirty the night before. Poor Mom had to get up at seven as usual, and they didn't finish till four. She phoned at noon and told me which train to take, where to get off, how to get to her office. I was there at three-thirty. She radiated all over the place, introducing me to everyone around. Actually, no one cared. They wanted to finish up and clear out, but I could tell they all like Mom, even the big boss.

Mom said she wasn't going to send me home without at least one night on the town, even though she was bushed. Somehow she got tickets to a musical at the last minute. Said not to ask what she paid; she hoped the show would be worth it. First we met Joe after work and walked through Central Park and around, then went to this Italian place we were supposed to go to Monday when I was late. It's the kind of place that has white tablecloths and real flowers and dark-haired dudes who shave twice a day and never smile. The theater was only a block away. The musical was good. I enjoyed it. About the barber of Fleet Street, who avenged himself for injustice by slitting the throats of his customers and giving their bodies to his girl friend to use in meat pies she sold. It was funny, but really it was about how cruel and mean humans can be to each other. His daughter sang in a high, sweet voice. Reminded me of Julie.

It was pouring and the wind was blowing when we left the theater, but as usual the sidewalks were crowded. We were hurrying to the subway station when I hear this bloodcurdling scream. After a few seconds another. Nobody paid any attention. I felt like the only hearing person in a world of unhearing shapes moving quickly through the rain. I peered into the murk and made out this guy about my age carrying an armful of books. He walked and he yelled. "Don't look at him," Mom whispered, but the guy's eyes met mine. There was no message. Blank stare. Was he suffering, or was he high, or was he completely out of it? I looked over my shoulder to see if I could get a clue. "Don't turn around!" Mom commanded. "You never know what they might do," Joe said. The guy disappeared into the murk, and the screams got fainter, and then I didn't hear them.

In Del Amo people would have looked. They would have given the guy a wide berth, but they would have acknowledged his existence by looking at him. Somehow that silly game Julie and I played about the footprints came into my mind. How can you be sure you are living if no one looks at you? You don't leave footprints on concrete.

This morning Joe drove us to the airport. He lives just around the corner from Mom. I thought he came with us Monday after the game to see us home and then had to go across town somewhere, but he's in the neighborhood. They met at that rinky-dink supermarket over the onions. He probably cracked Mom up with one of his corny jokes.

We ate breakfast at Kennedy. Mom was tired and weepy,

and neither of us had much to say. We had said it all Friday night. To fill up the silence, Joe told a long, complicated story about his troubles with the ignition system of his Datsun to the air over my left shoulder. When he escaped to get some cigarettes, Mom said, "Isn't he funny? He's still scared to death of you." She lit up with one of her thousand watters. "We're so good for each other. You do like him, don't you, Roger?" I said sure to the air over *her* left shoulder. "I'm sorry you didn't get to know him better. Come back this summer, honey. I still have the money, you know." I said I might have to study. She smiled. "And there's Julie. I hope you and she find a lot of happiness together." Then she reached for my hand. "Roger, remember what you promised Friday night. *Anytime*, day or night. Don't do anything till we talk. Keep calling until you reach me. Promise, Roger?" I promised and squeezed her hand tight.

Joe came back with his cigarettes, and it was time to leave. We walked over to the boarding gate, and Mom started crying when we hugged and kissed good-bye. Joe grabbed my hand and pumped it, saying, "Well, Champ, you coming back?"

"Does a snake have hips?" I said, grinning at Mom. She brightened up.

"Does a chicken have lips?" she said.

"Does a bear crap in the woods?" Joe boomed out, clapping me on the back.

"Isn't he the greatest?" Mom asked Joe, hugging me again.

"He's got a very good personality, only not for a human being," Joe said, which started Mom giggling and crying at the same time. Even though he's a real cornball, I liked him all of a sudden.

It occurs to me as I sit here looking out into the clouds, writing this all down, reliving the past week—it occurs to me that one act has ended. Finished. No going back. Don't know what the next one will be like—comedy or tragedy or what. Don't know if Julie and I will make it, if the tutoring will take, if Dad will meet me halfway—

I'm tired. I'm going to sleep now.

Forty minutes from LAX. I wonder if she will be at the field. She may not even have gotten my letter yet. I mailed it Wednesday. I should have waited till I got home so I could tell by her face what she is thinking, and I wouldn't have had that hassle with Mom. She's always getting me into one mess or another. I can't understand why I was in such a big sweat to answer her.

And Dad. And Vanessa. And Lou. I wish this flight would never end.

I am back in my room. They got me a new clock but no radio. Everything was neat till I started to unpack. There were even flowers on the bureau.

I had to interrupt my unpacking to write in here. This journal has been my best friend through some pretty rough times.

I was glad that only Dad met me at the airport. Gave me a bear hug like the one he gave me when I left. Looked me over and told me I'm getting tall. Then in a nasty, mocking tone he asked me if Mom set me straight, solved my problems, got me on the right track. I shrugged and changed the subject. Asked if Pippa had missed me. He said not that he could tell. "Think you want to live in New York?" he asked me, bringing the subject right back. Not right away, I said. He seemed to relax. Kept his arm around me all the way to the luggage claim. Maybe Mom is right. He asked where she works, where she lives, is she going with anyone. I said yes. Did I meet him? I nodded.

"Probably fat and bald and old enough to be her father," he sneered.

"Actually, he's six-four with thick curly black hair," I told him. I mean why does he have to put her down every time he mentions her? "And she's really off the juice for good this time," I told him.

"We'll see," he said, sour and stubborn.

Pippa was sitting like a statue in the van, ears erect, eyes fastened on us. When Dad unlocked the door, her ears went down and she moaned and raked me with her paw. When I got in, she jumped into my lap, gave me two kisses on the hand, and went to sleep. So I know she missed me. That's her way. Laid back.

When we got out of the airport traffic mess, Dad cleared his throat and asked if I'm ready to settle down to my school work. I said yes. He cleared his throat again, looked at me a second, then said, "What I can't understand is why you didn't level with me. Why did you give me that cock-and-bull story about the guy on crutches—and then he had V.D.? Did you really expect me to believe that baloney?"

I squirmed and looked out the window. It *was* a stupid story. "I promised I wouldn't tell who the girl was, and you would have made me tell," I told him.

"I would not have. A girl gets in trouble, her boyfriend runs out on her, she doesn't want her parents to know—I can understand that. It was all this other baloney that made me think you were hiding more than her name."

"I didn't want Vanessa to know I didn't do it," I said.

"That's another thing I don't understand—"

"I tried to tell you. I guess I just can't talk to you any more."

His wrinkles deepened. We drove for a while without talking. Then he cleared his throat again (he was really nervous) and said, "I told Lou that from now on it would be better if Vanessa used her car and you used the van. That way . . ."

I wanted to hug him the way I used to when I was a little kid, but of course I didn't. He was driving, for one thing, and for another, he wouldn't have liked it. So I only said, "O.K. That's cool." Then I asked, "What's with VID?"

"Well, we're hanging in there," he said, looking old and tired. "Mostly resales. The people who can't afford to keep vans because they lost their jobs or something are selling them to people who can't afford new ones, and they want modifications . . . and some woman wants to convert a van to a mobile beauty shop. And we're negotiating to combine with a guy who outfits tractor cabs. Of course, we're not going to move to the new house . . ."

"Is that dude my age still working for you?" I asked.

"No."

"Could I have his job?"

That question gave Dad a jolt. "What brought that on?" I didn't answer. I had stuck my neck out. I figured now it was his turn. "Why don't you look somewhere else? You need to get out on your own."

"I don't know how to do anything. You're my father, you ought to teach me."

He thought about that. Finally he said, "O.K. We'll give it a try. But you have to get those grades cleared up. That's the first priority. Understand?" I nodded. "I'll expect a full day's work from you. No goofing off!"

"I know!" I yelled at him so loud that Pippa grumbled. Why should he expect me to goof off?

When we got home, Lou kissed me and said, "Roger, let's give it a try. Let's act as if we're friends and see what happens." I shrugged and said O.K.

It depends on her and Vanessa. I'm not looking for trouble. I ran into the creep upstairs. I think she had been crying. I figured I'd go for broke and even give her a try, so I asked, "How was Lawndale?" She went into her room and slammed the door without answering. Something new has definitely been added.

Lou made a terrific Easter dinner. Ham and a lot of good stuff. Vanessa ate and sulked. Dad and Lou tossed names at me. World Trade Center? No. U.N.? No. Lincoln Center? No. Any of the museums? No.

"What the hell *did* you do?" my father asked.

I told him that I went to Yankee Stadium and Chinatown and Little Italy and saw a musical, *Sweeny Todd*, that I had a bad cold and it rained most of the week. After a couple pieces of lemon pie I came up here to put my stuff away, but when I went to the closet and started to hang shirts and pants from the high bar, all the memories came rushing back—

I have to go now. I wonder if she'll be there.

I ran to the field with the paper bag with the toads in one hand and the leash in the other. I was in such a sweat that I didn't allow Pippa any smells or marking squats. I tripped over her leash in the middle of Sepulveda and almost fell flat on my face just as the signal changed.

Of course, Julie wasn't there. I let Pippa off the leash in the eucalyptus grove and leaned against a tree where I could check out Maple Street, expecting to see her any second. I was so eager I hugged the damn tree. I tried to remember when I first knew I loved her. It seems as if I'd loved her all my life. It's hard to realize that I ever considered her a squeaky wart, a pest. So much was going on in my life that I was getting hooked without knowing. The abortion mess, Dad, Vanessa, me getting shipped off to New York.

My mind wandered. Was it only yesterday that I was in New York with Mom and Joe? Now, instead of crowded, narrow streets with the sky cut into narrow strips far away, I am looking at messy weeds dripping sunshine, and the sky is bright blue and comes almost to the ground.

Again I stare up the block on Maple Street. Maple Street is empty. My high drains away.

I start walking down the road, head down, hands in pockets, alone, the way I always have been. Over there Pippa is poised on three legs, head cocked, listening for gophers and mice. She has forgotten I have been away. At this moment she has probably forgotten that I am alive. The oil pumps are squeaking and rocking as always. Ahead of me a faint dust cloud follows a pickup truck. Not one thing that I see gives a damn that I have been through a hell of a time, have been to New York and back, that I love Julie Bierre. Least of all her. She isn't here. She is sending me a strong message. The message is, "Cool it, kid."

Then why did she write the poem? Why did she say I am

a fine human being? How do I know? All I know is I wish she had left me alone. I hurl the biggest rocks I can find at an oil pump. They bounce off the chain-link fence, ineffectively. I viciously clip Pippa on the flank causing her to yip and come running to me in confusion. When I ignore her, she follows me, dejected. I clump along in a vile mood.

Then I hear this fantastic squeak. "Roger! Wait up!"

And there she is, running toward me, just the way I dreamed, golden with sunshine, smiling, arms open, hair whipping around. I almost have a coronary.

"Here! I got them in Chinatown!" I screech, holding out the crumpled paper bag, as soon as she is in reaching distance.

She removes first one toad, then the other from the bag, carefully unwrapping the Chinese newspapers. "Horny toads!" she squeaks, mounting one on top of the other in her hand. "Lovers!"

I grab her around the neck and pull her to me. I kiss her adorable flat nose, her cheeks, her eyebrows, her forehead, but she is struggling, pushing against me to get away. I drop my arms as if she were on fire. I'm thinking, She doesn't like me. I'm not doing it right. I want to run away again.

"You're too rough. You're choking me," Julie says. "Like this." She places my arms around her waist, takes my face in her hands, and gently places those ripe, juicy lips on my dry, thirsty mouth.

We didn't leave the field till after dark. We'd fool around and talk and fool around and talk and fool around. The sun went down, and we were still walking and talking and fooling around. We must have made ten trips around the field. The dogs couldn't figure out what was going on.

Nobody was here when I got back. I'm glad. I phoned Julie, and we talked for half an hour. We had to cut it short because she got in trouble for being out after dark without telling her parents where she was. They're still mad.

I feel so good!!

Oh, Julie, my squeaky, flat-nosed angel, my weird, perfect love, I will see you tomorrow—and the next day—and the day after that—

I woke up a few hours ago. It was still dark. I never did fall back to sleep. After a while I could see the closet door in a blur, and the sky outside my window was lighter. A bird sang. Julie would know what kind. It was great watching the new day come in, the sky get brighter, the furniture gradually come out of the dark and take shape, the lines becoming sharp and clear. Now all the birds are singing, and though the sun is on the other side of the house and I can't see it, I know it's there because everything is golden.

I have to write in here because I am so full of Julie. She is so deep and crazy. And gorgeous.

On one of our trips around the field—near the spot where she gave me the poppy, as a matter of fact—we discussed her poem. I told her it was fantastic. She blushed and grinned, totally pleased that I thought it was good. She's pretty proud of it.

I said, "I wrote a poem, too, while I was in Brooklyn. It isn't as good as yours—" I tell her about my Disaster Data file. She smiles at the idea of DD. Then I recite my poem.

> "Fly to the east, fly to the west,
> Fly away, baby to the place you like best.
> Got news for you, baby, whatever your route,
> Disaster's gonna get you without a doubt."

It sounds glum and out of place with Julie radiating at me under the calm sunset sky.

"How can you be sure?" she asks.

"Everything I read and hear and see points that way," I tell her.

"But how can you be sure?" she repeats. "Look at all the forces and elements we don't even know about, and all the accidents that haven't even happened. By the law of averages, half of them have to work out, don't they? Look what happened to us because of those big slobs with rifles. We met each other. . . . I mean even for the whole world things work out sometimes, right? *All* the dreadful things can't happen— I mean we probably have a fifty percent chance of making it, maybe even better!"

It is getting dark, and all I can see is the faint gleam of her eyes, but I'm getting fantastic shocks from her bod next to me. I think of Joe and say, "Life, death, who cares as long as you're healthy." But she doesn't laugh. "I mean, what's so special about a fourth-rate planet in a third-rate solar system on the outskirts of a second-rate galaxy in some out-of-the-way corner of the universe?" I say, nuzzling at her ear.

"Prove it!" she says.

"Prove what?"

"How do you know where we are? We might be in the very middle of the whole schmeer. All the galaxies and nebulae and black holes they know about and all the galaxies and holes they don't know about!" She untangles herself from me and throws her arms open wide. "This very spot— the field, Del Amo, California, U.S.A., World—may be the hub of the universe, and everything may be revolving around us—flat and over and under and this way and that way—"

She is squeaking earnestly and flinging her arms about to indicate circles at various angles to form a sphere.

I grab her and kiss her, and I'll be damned if I can't feel the whole schmeer whirling and wheeling around me.

About the Author

HARRIETT LUGER is the author of *Chasing Trouble, The Elephant Tree,* and *Lauren,* published by The Viking Press. She was born in Vancouver, British Columbia, and received a B.A. degree in English literature from the University of California in Los Angeles.

Ms. Luger lives in Torrance, California, with her husband, who is a botanist, and a dog named Pippa.